DRRR!! 4

RYOHGO NARITA

ILLUSTRATION BY
SUZUHITO YASUDA

"Why am I following his orders and cooking him food…?"

"…Maybe I should slip some poison in."

Namie Yagiri

Erika Karisawa

"You've heard of otaku cars? I can do otaku *food.* It'll look like an anime character."

Emilia

"The remaining steps are simply to mix in the gunpowder and perform the ritual of ignition. The food will cook from the inside, just like in a microwave oven. Hee-hee!"

Anri Sonohara

"Um, I don't suppose I could use a katana…to peel…potatoes…?"

Celty Sturluson

"…If it were a crab omelet, I could make that…"

Mika Harima

"My cooking skill exists only for Seiji's sake! So if you think it tastes good, thank Seiji instead!"

VOLUME 4

Ryohgo Narita
ILLUSTRATION BY Suzuhito Yasuda

YEN
ON

NEW YORK

DURARARA!!, Volume 4
RYOHGO NARITA,
ILLUSTRATION BY SUZUHITO YASUDA

Translation by Stephen Paul
Cover art by Suzuhito Yasuda

DURARARA!!
© RYOHGO NARITA 2008
All rights reserved.
Edited by ASCII MEDIA WORKS
First published in 2006 by KADOKAWA CORPORATION, Tokyo.
English translation rights arranged with KADOKAWA CORPORATION, Tokyo,
through Tuttle-Mori Agency, Inc., Tokyo.

English translation © 2016 by Yen Press, LLC

Yen On
1290 Avenue of the Americas
New York, NY 10104

Visit us at yenpress.com
facebook.com/yenpress
twitter.com/yenpress
yenpress.tumblr.com

First Yen On Edition: July 2016

Yen On is an imprint of Yen Press, LLC.
The Yen On name and logo are trademarks of Yen Press, LLC.

Library of Congress Cataloging-in-Publication Data

Names: Narita, Ryōgo, 1980– author. | Yasuda, Suzuhito, illustrator. | Paul, Stephen (Translator), translator.
Title: Durarara!! / Ryohgo Narita, Suzuhito Yasuda, translation by Stephen Paul.
Description: New York, NY : Yen ON, 2015–
Identifiers: LCCN 2015041320| ISBN 9780316304740 (v. 1 : pbk.) |
    ISBN 0316304743 (v. 1 : pbk.) | ISBN 9780316304764 (v. 2 : pbk.) |
    ISBN 031630476X (v. 2 : pbk.) | ISBN 9780316304771 (v. 3 : pbk.) |
    ISBN 0316304778 (v. 3 : pbk.) | ISBN 9780316304788 (v. 4 : pbk.) |
    ISBN 0316304786 (v. 4 : pbk.)
Subjects: | CYAC: Tokyo (Japan)—Fiction. | BISAC: FICTION /
Science Fiction / Adventure.
Classification: LCC PZ7.1.N37 Du 2015 | DDC [Fic]—dc23 LC record
    available at http://lccn.loc.gov/2015041320

ISBNs: 978-0-316-30478-8 (paperback)
978-0-316-30495-5 (ebook)

10 9 8 7 6 5 4 3 2 1

RRD-C

Printed in the United States of America

Stop me if you've heard this one.

Like us, the city wants to take a holiday sometimes.

Just like an office worker pulling overtime shifts or a student studying hard on a Sunday night instead of kicking back and watching *Sazae-san* before school resumes the next morning.

But, of course, as long as there are people, a city doesn't have time to sleep.

Still, there are times the city gets to relax.

But every day off isn't just about lying in bed past noon, is it?

The city likes to watch the people walking its streets and toys with them.

That's how the city enjoys its days off.

Let's take Ikebukuro, for instance. If you get wrapped up in something odd...

Just assume that the city is toying with you.

And if you can do that...

Try to play along.

—Excerpt from the afterword of Shinichi Tsukumoya, author of Media Wax's Ikebukuro travel guide, *Ikebukuro Strikes Back*

Sazae-san holds the Guinness World Record as Japan's longest-running anime. It aired Sunday nights between six thirty and seven.

PROLOGUE
RUMOR

"The murder-machine philosopher."

Those were the words the man used to describe him.

"I happen to think epithets like that are rather trite, but if you had to put a giant title on him, like the tabloid rags at the supermarket, that's what you'd expect to see. He's a hit man who carries out his work like a machine, but there's an odd aesthetic he follows."

This machinelike hit man, said to be the seventh-most-feared professional killer in Russia, was indeed inhuman in his manner.

Reputedly, his victims numbered over eighty, and his hits all shared a certain unique feature: He did not prepare any murder weapon beforehand but used whatever was on hand at the scene of the killing.

If his target had a gun, he would twist their arm until they shot themselves in the forehead.

If it was in a kitchen, he could use a knife or even a rolling pin or the ice in the freezer as a weapon.

The ex-military hooligan murdered in a bank had his throat slit by a fresh stack of bills.

He was a hit man of considerable legend—but no one knew his name.

Nor did they know where to find him or how to make reliable contact.

His appearance was unknown. The only way they knew he had killed was by his method.

"Isn't it fascinating? If anyone in Russia is looking for a hit man, they just cast out for one and hire him. So this guy goes looking for 'people looking for a hit man.' He hears about them and takes it upon himself to contact his prospective client."

The hit man would take a job, complete it in short order, then leave and change his name, never to meet his client again.

In other words, he became famous without a name, only the vague profile that appeared to fit a single person based on the similarity of the methods of murder.

"Well, it seems this hit man...has come to our country now. Apparently, they finally uncovered his identity back home, and now the associates of his victims are after him. His job while he's here is to eliminate two men who stole a huge secret from a Russian group a few years back," the information agent chattered happily.

The dead-eyed woman he was talking to was busy filing papers and showed no interest in the topic of hired killers.

"From what some people say, he could take down a special forces agent or two without a sneak attack—in fact, they could try to sneak up on *him* and he'd still win... Are you listening?"

"Dunno."

Whether she thought the story too unrealistic or accepted it as fact but just didn't care, the woman had offered no responses to his story other than tepid *ahh*s and *uh-huh*s. The information dealer shook his head in pity and said, "You really are a tremendously boring woman, Namie. Your brother's never going to take an interest in you at this rate."

"I don't need him to. I'm satisfied just watching Seiji from behind."

"Well, isn't that creepy."

"I find it quite pleasant. It makes me happy just to think of Seiji's face and know that I'm breathing the air on the same planet as him. But not satisfied," she said, a look of sheer bliss on her face. It was definitely creepy.

The woman named Namie returned to her usual stone-faced expression and asked her employer, "And what do you expect to do, talking about some hit man who might as well have popped out of a comic book? Has all this Headless Rider and demon blade nonsense turned your brain into manga, too?"

"I won't deny it," he said, smiling smoothly and reaching for a can of beer on the table. "It turns out those two on the run he's looking for are a black man and a white man."

"..."

"They run a sushi restaurant in Ikebukuro now. But I'm not sure if the hit man is aware of that or not."

Whether by coincidence or intention, on the very day that this conversation happened, the "murder-machine philosopher" arrived in Ikebukuro.

♂♀

Just at the time the Russian murder-machine came to Japan, the country was swarming with its own shadows.

Only it was happening before the eyes of the entire nation on TV—hardly what one expects when it comes to shadows.

"This is the hotel where the latest incident occurred," the reporter was saying, motioning gravely to the building behind him. It was very obviously a love hotel—the kind you reserve by the hour. He continued to report the details with the utmost gravity. "The attack happened before dawn this morning. When screams issued from a second-floor room, employees rushed to the scene to find an unconscious woman spattered with blood and a deceased man whose body had been grievously injured."

The killer Hollywood.

That was the Internet-given nickname of the suspect in the serial killings. In fact, there were no true suspects in a concrete sense.

A witness to the first of the string of murders described the attacker as "a person wearing a lifelike wolf mask." There were no direct witnesses of the next killing, but someone did spot a "half-fish man, like you'd see in the movies," jumping from the third floor of the hotel where the murder happened, then scampering away.

On the news segment covering the latest killing, the woman who witnessed the entire attack said that "a monster with a dinosaur face scooped out the victim's heart with its bare hands." Sure enough, the hotel's security cameras showed a figure with a dinosaur face running off like some wild beast.

When one of the investigators watched the footage, he remarked, "It reminds me of one of those South American chupacabra videos," an observation that was so accurate, it earned a round of tasteless snorts and chuckles.

That was a sign of how fake and yet realistic the video was.

The common feature of all the killer's victims was the remarkable destruction they suffered, *without losing any limbs*. One victim's flesh was stripped from all over his body; one man's genitals, tongue, and partial spine were cut out; and one victim's face was crushed.

The killer was nicknamed Hollywood after the various movie-monster forms taken for each different appearance. The media avoided picking up that moniker, out of fears of complaints from the movie and tourism industries, but on the Net, the legend spread far and wide.

There was once an American couple who performed a series of stick-ups in various costumes, but the culprit in this case was much, much more than just a costume.

After all, Hollywood had the viciousness, the ferocity, and the sheer wall- and door-destroying bare-handed power of an actual monster.

Without any leads on a suspect or hints at a motive, the only option was to recoil in fear of the killer's potential appearance. Many of those a safe distance from the scenes of rampage found a kind of perverse entertainment from the show that was Hollywood's trail of destruction.

So it was that the serial killings, all happening around the capital, were the biggest source of gossip of the day. Hollywood's presence—if not identity—was made known around the nation.

And tonight, the killer prowled the streets of Ikebukuro.

$$\male\female$$

Two shadows arrived in Ikebukuro, ironically on the very same day.

Through fate or coincidence, they crossed paths on the night streets.

Whatever happened between them is unknown.

The only certainty is that they each held hostility toward the other.

Two of the worst people on the planet met, found murderous intent, and set about to end the other.

Ikebukuro was flooded in callous, unthinking malice, and a blood-bath to eclipse the infamous Night of the Ripper two months earlier began to swallow the city into its grotesque maw…

♂♀

Well, it should have.

The shining neon lights of the commercial district set the night scene in Ikebukuro.

In a park, slightly off the center of town, there was a *plock* sound, like a giant wooden fish drum from a Buddhist temple being slammed by a train.

Right after the hit man and the killer first faced off, the hit man picked up the nearest object he could use as a murder weapon, like he always did.

On a bench nearby sat some rather unsavory-looking young men.

They looked like your typical street toughs, eating their rice ball dinner from a plastic convenience store bag. For some reason, there was an out-of-place briefcase sitting next to them, and the hit man grabbed it without hesitation.

It was instantaneous.

So fast that it was beyond the processing power of the typical human being, with flowing precision and maximum efficiency.

The murder-machine hit man grabbed the briefcase like a gust of wind—and, with perfect timing, perfect angle, and perfect velocity, swung it toward Hollywood's chin.

But just before the briefcase intersected with the killer, Hollywood's manual chop entered from an unnatural angle and tore through the briefcase as if it were soft tofu.

Papers, bills, a broken pen, and the drops of ink from within it sprayed outward.

With honed reflexes, each combatant caught sight of the phenomenon in slow motion. They each had a perfect view of the other.

Next to them sat the dumbfounded hooligans. Determining that they posed no threat, the two killers instead focused entirely on the other.

They had to be evenly matched. Even if they weren't, it was the kind of fight in which victory or defeat could be determined by any number of variables. Their brains subconsciously worked away at the calculations, but their conscious minds stayed perfectly focused.

The two killers, alike in many ways, launched themselves into an orgy of slaughter.

Launched themselves entirely and unfortunately.

They threw their concentration, their caution, their everything into that moment.

Which is why the two murderers failed to notice that of the two owners of the briefcase sitting dumbfounded on the bench, one was wearing a bartender's outfit, *despite not working at a bar.*

As they were outsiders to Ikebukuro, they also did not realize that there were people in Ikebukuro one must *never pick a fight with.*

People whom no one should ever, ever, ever challenge to a fight, no matter if they were a hit man, or a serial killer, or a president, or an alien, or a vampire, or a headless monster.

Hence, the advent of the wooden *plock.*

Right before the sound, the two noticed something.

Just as they were about to make contact, out of the corner of their eyes, they caught the unnatural silhouette of the bartender, his mouth twitching, lifting the park bench in one hand.

Having pulled the bolted-down bench straight out of the ground, the man in the bartender outfit bellowed, "Why, you...*little sneak thieves!*"

He swung the bench at them.

It was a swing worthy of a baseball slugger, if you ignored that he did it with only one hand.

The weapon with size and speed that transcended common sense caught the murder-machine on his nose as he tried to evade, destroying part of his face and delivering a shock to his brain and spine.

The park bench hurtled through the air toward Hollywood in an instant. The killer tensed instinctively in defense but was literally tossed into the air, flying completely out of the park and out of sight.

In American cartoons, characters were often knocked clean out of a scene by a hammer, and that was how Hollywood departed this one. The murder-machine's wits were similarly knocked right out of his skull.

As he picked up the bills and notes that spilled out of the broken briefcase, the dreadlocked man who didn't take part in the fight noted, "You won't need to go for a second shot, Shizuo."

The man with the park bench raised for the finishing blow, Shizuo Heiwajima, looked down at the immobile Caucasian and begrudgingly returned the bench to its former position.

"Dammit. What do these sneak thieves expect me to do, carry this cash around in my hands all night?"

"Um…do you really think they were sneak thieves?" the dreadlocked man wondered, but Shizuo was already walking toward the exit of the park.

"I'm going to go see if the Don Quixote has any briefcases," he said calmly and abruptly, referring to a nearby discount store. Shizuo raced off to the park exit.

As he watched his money-counting partner trot away, the man shook his dreads and wondered, "Who would challenge Shizuo to a fight in this neighborhood? They must be from out of town."

He looked down at the white man with half pity and half dismay. "Remember this: A bartender's outfit in this town is a bigger warning signal than a red light. Too late to put that knowledge to use, though," he said to the likely unconscious man, then turned on his heel. "By way of apology for the overboard treatment, I won't tell the cops about you. So don't hold a grudge against me, got it? And if you want to live, don't hold a grudge against the bartender guy, either."

The man briefly wondered about the red-eyed zombie that Shizuo knocked out with the bench, then waved his hand and said to the both of them, "Well, anyway. That's what kind of city this is. Enjoy your stay."

"Welcome to Ikebukuro. You both looked pretty impressive. You just had bad luck."

A hit man and a killer appeared in the city.

But that was all.

Two sources of violence were instantly crushed by an even greater violence.

The chance meeting of those murderous figures should have been a big deal, but it was merely toyed with.

Ikebukuro slowly enjoyed its holiday.

It watched the various organisms contained within itself and their activities...

And the city stretched out to relax.

DR RR 1 2 3 4 !

CHAPTER 1
DAIOH TV, SPECIAL PROGRAM
IKEBUKURO'S 100-DAY FRONT

"The city of Ikebukuro knows no rest," said the ominous narration on the TV, displaying the night city as filmed from inside a moving police car. "Since the serial assaults known as the Night of the Ripper two months ago, the populace has lived in fear. Yet Ikebukuro's night continues to writhe with life."

It was the kind of special program often shown at the end of the year, where film crews accompanied a police patrol to catch the decisive moment in an exciting case to show to the viewers in their peaceful homes.

In most cases, these weren't shocking, nation-crumbling incidents, but simple local brawls, unlicensed or drunken driving, stolen vehicle crackdowns, and other everyday events that wouldn't even get listed in a newspaper's local safety section.

But because of the special immediacy of video footage, the programs succeeded in implanting a specific idea into the heads of its peaceful viewers: "Crime is nearby, and the city at night is dangerous."

There was just one difference from the usual pattern in Daioh TV's special program.

"On these streets, the very veins of our city, an eerie shadow dances in the darkness…"

The picture cut to the start of a now-famous video clip.

"A motorcycle entirely in black, with no headlight or license plate. This alone qualifies it as a public danger on the street."

As usual, the place was Ikebukuro at night. But there was something different to the footage this time, something *off*.

In the center of the screen was a black motorcycle, racing down the street after a car. As the narrator said, it had no headlight or plate, making the vehicle look like a 3-D representation of a solid black silhouette.

There was the sound of gunfire, and the helmet of the bike's rider shot backward, raising off its shoulders for just an instant. But it returned to its original position just as quickly.

It was creepy enough, the way it seemed to snap back into place with black rubber bands—but the real problem was what that momentary dislocation revealed.

The instant the helmet rose upward…there was nothing beneath it.

It wasn't a trick of the eye, or camouflage from black hair, or anything of that sort.

The camera caught a clear glimpse of the shooter's car in the space between the helmet and the rider's neck.

The sight could be succinctly described thusly: "The rider on the pitch-black bike has no head above the neck."

A black shadow that extended from the empty cross section of neck grabbed the base of the helmet and pulled it back into place.

It was already suspicious footage to start with, but the very cheap suspicion of it all, when combined with the straight-faced genre of news reporting, gave the scene an eerie reality.

There was one other unsettling feature about the rider. A tool, pure black with no highlight, as thick and pure as a midsummer shadow, that swung around just before the man shot at the rider.

It was too twisted and hideous to call a "weapon."

The pole, a good ten feet long at least—twice the height of the rider—was connected to a sickle blade just as long.

The first instant the cameraman caught sight of it, he mistook it for the ostentatious insignia flags that motorcycle gangs waved as they rode. Such was the size of the pole the mystery rider held.

The scythe, which looked like the one Death held on his tarot card, was huge and menacing and as black, black, black as a shadow against a wall cast by a car's headlights.

"Is it a social outcast gleefully seeking to shock the public? A daring member of some motorcycle gang? Even the police have no answer yet."

The answer was clearly beyond those tame descriptors, but the dignity of a serious news program prohibited them from using words like *monster* or *ghoul*. Yet it was clear from a simple glance that this was not an attention seeker or a biker gang member or even a human being—it was *something else*.

Many people could bring themselves to recognize that this was "something beyond the realm of human understanding," but none of them could *accept* it.

Which was why half of the media was desperate to attach some kind of meaning to it. The other half got busy trying to bring acceptance to the unaccepting and made a business of it.

It was a true example of the grotesque brought to modern times.

People on opposing sides—those who sought to bring about another cyclical boom of interest in the occult and those who denied its otherworldly cause—set about to reveal the true nature of the Headless Rider for their own ends.

Thus, the media found itself chasing after the mysterious Headless Rider. Among the journalists, some claimed it was a "true monster."

The footage from the TV cameras was so vivid, it looked for all the world to see as though the rider's head was gone.

The image was too raw to be faked, and this peculiar persuasiveness led to the propagation of a rumor: that the Headless Rider existed in the space between reality and urban legend, a being born of the spread of public rumor itself.

An urban legend that anyone could spot if they just lurked around Ikebukuro for a few days.

On this night, the liminal being was being pursued by many such curious onlookers.

But without definitive proof for the public to see, the Headless Rider became a prototypical "modern mystery" with no actual answer, an otherwise accepted part of society.

*   *   *

As for the mystery herself…

She was stuck at a part-time job in a corner of Nerima Ward.

♂♀

Nerima Ward

Bright light hugged pale skin.

Beneath a light so powerful it seemed to blend the boundary between reality and fantasy lay a woman's naked body. Two shapely mounds rose above finely chiseled abs, and a finger frolicked fishlike through the soft cleavage.

The finger belonged to another woman, her blond hair shining in the vivid light. She was dressed as a doctor or researcher, and her golden eyes stood out on her young face, somehow clashing with the white coat that covered her body.

It wasn't just the uniform that clashed with her face, but the body beneath it, which was even more curvaceous and inflammatory than the naked one on the bed. The uniformed woman was unconsciously writhing and squirming with pleasure.

If the blond woman's body was a personification of pure, heady lust, then the woman on the table exuded a more wholesome eros. Together, the two figures shone in stark, desirable profile within the light.

The finger tracing the naked woman's breasts slid down to her abdomen to lightly circle her navel.

If these were the only details examined, it would be quite an erotic sight, but one particular oddity ruined the effect and turned the scene into something extremely abnormal.

In fact, it was so unlikely and freakish that that the word *oddity* was wholly inadequate to describe it.

Because the naked woman lying on the bed had no head.

The cross section at her neck was so smooth and natural that it looked like less of a severance than that there had never been a head there to begin with. The cross section was shrouded in black shadow that covered up the esophagus and backbone that would normally be visible there.

But if that odd shadow was ignored, it looked like nothing more than an examination of a dead body—a white doctor performing an autopsy on a mutilated corpse.

The absence of a head turned it into an utterly unsexy scene. But when the woman in the lab coat took her hands off the headless "body" and spoke, her voice had no hint of *either* husky lust or scientific examination.

"I have finished to conclusion! There is much thanks for your accomplicing!"

Her bizarre version of Japanese was followed by something even more jarring.

The headless woman's hand writhed and issued a black *something*. It was less of a gas than a kind of liquid that seemed to blend into the air.

The substance was the kind of black that actually stole the light it absorbed, closer to shadow or darkness than a color. This shadow issued forth and then enveloped the entirety of the naked body, clamping to the skin in a way that was nothing short of sentient.

The woman dressed in white watched this process with obvious interest, but no surprise in the least. In no more than a few seconds, the headless woman on the bed went from totally naked to covered in a pitch-black riding suit.

The one element that hadn't changed was her total lack of a head. She sat up from the bed, not bothered in the least by the absence of a skull, and picked up a PDA sitting on the nearby desktop.

The bizarre creature coolly typed a message into the device and showed the screen to the woman in the lab coat.

"It's not 'accomplicing.' What you meant to say is 'cooperation.'"

"Oh dear. I have apologized. I am terrifyingly sorryful."

"...Well, I can tell you know enough to read kanji... You aren't speaking this messed-up Japanese for the sake of being memorable, are you?"

"That is totally undeniable lack of truth. Ring-a-ding-dub," she said with an innocent smile.

The Headless Rider shrugged and typed, *"I can't tell if you're confirming or denying that accusation... Listen, Emilia. Just give me this week's pay. Also, I think you meant 'Rub-a-dub-dub.' 'Ring-a-ding-ding' is the theme the Robapan bakery trucks play."*

"It is so shrewd and abacusing of you to leap right to reward. It is better to improve cuteness by demure shyness, such as the traditional Japanese way, yes?"

"How can I be a traditional Japanese woman when I'm from Ireland?"

The woman the Headless Rider called Emilia pouted and cried, "Now you are Ikebukuroican! And it is appreciated to the nth degree to call me Mother. Mommy is also allowed. Mamma mia."

"Uh...well, I'll admit that I'm considering my future with Shinra, but the concrete topic of marriage is a ways off. Besides, you're younger than both me and Shinra, so calling you mother would be weird."

She twisted her body in apparent shyness, but without cheeks for blushing, the motion made her look more like a writhing zombie with its head blown off.

"Just give me my pay! It's the only reason I'm going through with these unpleasant medical tests. And what was that last physical examination for?"

"Oh, the boiled-egg skin is so beautiful and smooth, I simply wished to engage in pleasures of fondling closely."

"...I'll pretend not to be angry if you just give me my week's worth of money."

"Yes, yes, please to be calm. Haste make waste, broke as joke," Emilia said distractingly and produced a heavy envelope.

Inside the brown manila folder, which had "Payment—Celty Sturluson" handwritten on it, was a stack of a hundred ten-thousand-yen bills, each with the face of Yukichi Fukuzawa on it.

The Headless Rider utilized a myriad of little shadow tendrils to quickly count the total, then happily turned and typed a message with a few extra symbols into the PDA.

"Looks good! ☆ Thanks for your business! ♪"

With an absolutely outrageous week's pay in hand, the headless woman, Celty Sturluson, trotted gleefully out of the lab.

When she reached the underground garage, Celty turned to the motorcycle parked in the corner. It was totally hidden by a rain cover, but oddly enough, the material was not the usual silver, but the same featureless black that covered Celty's body.

She put a hand to the cover, and it dissipated instantly, the tiny black particles melting into thin air. The action looked like some kind of sorcery, but Celty sat on the bike without a second thought and put the helmet hanging on the handlebars onto her neck.

A Headless Rider in the dark of night, riding a black bike without lights or license plate.

Without the slightest shred of understanding of the effect this combination had on the rest of society, or of the mystery her own existence posed, Celty gunned the engine with a sound like a horse whinnying and rode out into Ikebukuro.

♂♀

Celty Sturluson was not human.

She was a type of fairy commonly known as a dullahan, found from Scotland to Ireland—a being that visits the homes of those close to death to inform them of their impending mortality.

The dullahan carried its own severed head under its arm, rode on a two-wheeled carriage called a Coiste Bodhar pulled by a headless horse, and approached the homes of the soon to die. Anyone foolish enough to open the door was drenched with a basin full of blood. Thus the dullahan, like the banshee, made its name as a herald of ill fortune throughout European folklore.

One theory claimed that the dullahan bore a strong resemblance to the Norse Valkyrie, but Celty had no way of knowing if this was true.

It wasn't that she *didn't* know. More accurately, she just couldn't remember.

When someone back in her homeland stole her head, she lost her memories of what she was. It was the search for the faint trail of her head that had brought her here to Ikebukuro.

Now with a motorcycle instead of a headless horse and a riding suit instead of armor, she had wandered the streets of this neighborhood for decades.

But ultimately, she had not succeeded at retrieving her head, and her memories were still lost. And she was fine with that.

As long as she could live with those human beings she loved and who accepted her, she could live the way she was now.

She was a headless woman who let her actions speak for her missing face and held this strong, secret desire within her heart.

That was Celty Sturluson in a nutshell.

♂♀

Highway, Ikebukuro

As she raced toward the center of the city, Celty eagerly contemplated the near future.

Wow, who'd have thought I'd make a million yen in short-term income in just a week? I should use this to buy Shinra some new glasses.

Shinra was the black-market doctor who was Celty's romantic partner and roommate. He was an odd fellow who loved her for both her mind *and* her appearance, and she loved him back with all of her heart.

The image of her beloved eccentric lighting up with joy made Celty even more excited. She considered other ways to spend the remainder.

I could use a new mini laptop... Oh, right, and I really need a new helmet.

The job she just left was a sudden, unexpected source of income, which made this windfall a bit of a personal bonus unrelated to savings.

She normally made her money as a courier, but nearly all of the proceeds from that business went to savings for the future.

This new venture started about a month ago, when she first met Emilia, who came to Ikebukuro following Shinra's father. Emilia worked for a major pharmaceutical company overseas and boldly demanded to play with Celty's body.

Naturally, Celty refused at first, only accepting with reluctance once she had been assured there would be only a minimum of open surgery or cell sampling and the only contact would come from female researchers.

But mostly, it was the amount of pay that Emilia mentioned that sealed the deal.

In the past, I would have no choice but to leave all of the money with

Shinra. But now you can buy pretty much anything with anonymity online. Long live modern civilization.

It was not a typical line of thought for an inhuman spook, but Celty was too busy indulging in crass materialism to care.

In my case, it's helpful that I don't need to spend money on my bike. All I need to buy are brushes to keep Shooter's mane in line. He even hates the idea of stickers on his body.

That had to be the nickname of her Coiste Bodhar. She patted the bike, which also happened to be her trusty headless steed. The normally silent motorcycle engine whinnied in apparent delight, startling nearby pedestrians.

Hee-hee, you adorable scamp, she thought, already looking forward to spending her million yen, the way a child looks forward to buying candy the day before a field trip.

I'll still have seven hundred thousand yen left over. Maybe I'll buy that DVD recorder I've been wanting. The kind that dubs straight from a video deck. Then, I'll have a more compact storage solution for all the episodes of Gatten, Mysterious Discoveries, TV Investigations, *Monday nine* PM *dramas,* Partner, Antique Appraisers, *and all the other shows I've been taping.*

Also, let's see... Right, I can buy some gourmet food for Shinra to eat. He did say he wanted to try sagohachi-*style pickled sandfish sometime. Is this even the right season for sandfish?*

In mid-April, sandfish season was long over. The bigger problem for Celty was how to cook the dish. Having no head naturally meant having no tongue. The shadow that her body produced functioned somewhat like a radar, giving her sight, hearing, and even smell through some means unknown.

But there was a problem: Because she didn't need to eat for whatever reason, she had no sense of taste and no way of knowing if the scents she was picking up were the same things Shinra smelled.

So if she followed a recipe when cooking, it might *look* right, but there was no way for her to check the actual flavor.

With long years of training, she had gradually learned how to cook certain egg-based dishes to Shinra's liking, such as crab omelets or scrambled eggs. But for other food, she could only make it by following the recipe to the letter, and given that she couldn't detect when she'd accidentally used sugar instead of salt, it was always a surprise until Shinra finally tasted it.

I ought to find a good cook and take serious lessons from them. I wonder…if Anri or Karisawa are any good at cooking? she wondered, thinking of her closest female acquaintances, but neither of them seemed to have that cooking air about them. Emilia wouldn't know the first thing about Japanese food, and the other women she knew were all the eccentric type.

I have a newfound respect for the housewife, the monster thought in admiration. She looked up at the night sky and shrugged. The stars were nearly invisible behind the light of the city. The only object that made its presence known was the moon.

I suppose being able to think about this topic is a sign that my life is good. Not that I was confident of that last month, after Emilia showed up…

By all accounts, Emilia was freeloading in their apartment, but she spent most of the week staying over at the lab, which meant she was almost never home.

Instead, the abnormality of that visit turned into everyday experiments, but that ended up with a minimum of suffering and more than enough reward to make up for it.

The light turned red and she came to a stop, reflecting on the sheer humanity of her life with relief.

This is it. This is what I wanted.

Peaceful days with the one she loved.

As an abnormal, headless knight, she understood just what a rare bliss that was and was acutely aware of the warmth enveloping her emotions.

In fact, I might just call Emilia "Mother" after all. I wonder how Shinra would react.

She felt a peaceful feeling come over her as she imagined her lover's flustered face and waited for the light to change.

But…

Humanity did not know or care of the goings-on in Celty's daily life.

It wanted nothing more than to plunge her into hell as the symbol of the abnormal.

*   *   *

"Excuse me, may I have a word?"

Hmm?

Celty made a show of swiveling her helmet around as her other-worldly senses focused on the surroundings. A portly man was holding out what looked like a mic toward her as she waited for the light.

Me? What does he want? Why is he holding a mic out into the middle of the street?

The man was standing on the other side of the guardrail, holding his mic over it into the road where she waited, a deadly serious look on his face.

"I'm Fukumi, a reporter for Daioh TV. I'd like to ask you some questions."

Oh no.

Celty noticed another man with a TV camera standing a slight distance away and even more men in plainclothes standing around beyond him. She understood Fukumi's intentions at once.

"We're currently filming for a news special here in Ikebukuro... I've noticed that your motorcycle has no headlight or license plate. This is clearly illegal, is it not?" the reporter asked, which was a perfectly correct observation. Unfortunately, the light was not going to turn green anytime soon.

Damn, I forgot that this is a long light.

In a way, it was rather silly that a motorcycle rider without a headlight or license plate was obeying a traffic light, but the reporter did not crack a smile. "May we assume that the Black Rider witnessed over the years is you? What is your purpose in engaging in such dangerous traffic activities?"

For an instant, the bike growled. It was a low, menacing *grrrl*, like an animal sending a warning signal. The reporter flinched momentarily, disturbed by the motorcycle's lack of an ordinary engine rumble, but he regained his cool immediately.

"Please tell us something. Are you aware that you're committing a crime?"

Oh... What do I do now? If I clam up, it'll only make me look worse to the rest of society.

It's not a huge deal to me, but I don't like the idea of those I associate with being treated like criminals, too... Then again, I can't possibly get licensed, and Shooter doesn't like wearing a headlight...

Celty was no closer to finding a solution to her quandary. As a courier, she had naturally been involved in ferrying items that ran afoul of the law. There was no denying that her vehicle broke a number of traffic regulations.

But that didn't mean she could turn around and say, *"Don't mind me, I'm just a monster anyway."*

...Hmm? Actually, I guess I could say that. If I give that news program some impossible footage, they won't be able to use the film, and if they did run it, the viewers would assume it was fake CG. And they've already filmed me once.

She decided to take out her PDA and type a message, showing it to the reporter.

"...? What is this? Um...what do you mean by this?"

Startled by her sudden response, the reporter look back and forth between the PDA screen and her helmet.

He couldn't be blamed. The message on the screen said:

"This is a horse, so it doesn't need a headlight or license plate."

"Is that supposed to be a jo... *Whaa—?!*" the reporter yelped, freezing up with shock.

The black motorcycle's silhouette writhed and morphed, growing to twice its previous size. It transformed from a mechanical shape to a biological one in a way that was clearly violating the laws of physics—and in a few seconds, it looked like a pitch-black horse.

But there was something wrong with this horse.

"A-aah...," the reporter cried again, not at the transformation, but the finished product. He couldn't be blamed for this.

The Headless Rider's beloved headlightless bike had faithfully carried over that particular detail.

The horse had no head.

Hee-hee! I haven't turned him into a horse since that time we went driving in the forests around Fuji, Celty thought proudly, as she stroked the abbreviated neck and looked back at the reporter. He was frozen in place, visibly trembling, but she didn't react any differently, leisurely typing a fresh message into the PDA.

"I believe you understand now. If you'll excuse me."

Horses are treated as light vehicles, just like bicycles, right? she wondered, as she resumed waiting for the light to change.

Anyone who saw that footage on the news would assume the TV station had lost the distinction between news reporting and action blockbuster movies. Perhaps that was actually the reason that mainstream society refused to report on anything unknown or otherworldly.

The crosswalk signal began to blink, which meant the light would turn green in just a few seconds. Celty stashed the PDA and considered how to leave the scene with maximum dramatic impact.

But then—

"Hey."

She felt a chill run down her back and through her heart.

"I'm talkin' to you, monster," said a familiar voice behind her. Celty's body had no blood running in it, but she still felt her heart jackhammering like a frog undergoing vivisection in science class.

Don't turn around.

Must turn around.

Instinct and reason sent conflicting warnings to Celty's body.

It was behind her. *Something* that could not be reasoned with.

The part of her that wanted to be sure and formulate a plan and the part of her that wanted to flee instantly faced off and sent tremendous turbulence through her mind.

She slowly, carefully turned her attention behind her, feeling her backbone creak.

It was a traffic patrol officer with a pleasant smile on his face, riding on a white police motorcycle. The very man who had once implanted fear into Celty's heart, wearing a smile that was half pleasure and half anger. He squeezed the handlebars.

"Did you know that even in a light vehicle, riding without a headlight is subject to penalty?"

The light turned green.

At the same time, it brought an end to Celty's brief era of peace—and launched a terrifying game of tag between monster and human.

Only in this case, the usual roles of predator and prey were reversed.

♂♀

A fierce animal cry ripped through Ikebukuro as Shooter trampled his massive hooves.

Celty squeezed the reins that had once been handlebars, completely forgetting to change her ride back into a motorcycle.

Shooter was something like a witch's familiar, a creature made by possessing and melding a dead horse and the wreckage of a carriage. When she came to Japan, she found a scrapyard and melded him with an old bike, which gave him a third form to use.

A simple headless horse.

The same headless horse pulling a carriage, if necessary.

And now, to fit in with modern society, a motorcycle without a headlight.

She didn't have time for the carriage now. Celty left the matter in her partner's powerful hooves—she was too busy trembling in fear of the patrol bike's exhaust on her tail.

Ahead, she saw that the light had turned red again. The cars on the cross street proceeded into the intersection, so leaping forward would surely cause an accident—if not initiated by herself, then by the drivers startled to see a headless horse leaping into traffic. And Celty wasn't so much of a monster that she'd allow that to happen.

Damn!

She checked that no one was on the crosswalk, then adeptly tugged at the reins, turning her steed around. As soon as their speed dropped, she felt a heavy, lurking pressure at her back, but there was no time to falter.

The Coiste Bodhar leaped forward and over the guardrail, its massive black form racing toward the side of the building.

The headless horse "landed" on the wall.

Shadows bloomed from each hoof, growing and fusing with the concrete surface. As if there was magic tape with powers beyond human understanding sticking the horse's legs to the surface, Shooter raced vertically up the side of the building.

"Hah! You won't get away from me that easily!" the officer shouted, not rattled in the least by this supernatural showing.

He spun the bike into a sudden 180-degree turn for an abrupt stop, watching Celty's path closely. She, on the other hand, was desperately searching for a way out as she felt his searing gaze from the ground below.

Oh, crap. Crap, crap, crap. This is bad. This is uncontrollably, severely, uncontrollably, incredibly, uncontrollably bad.

Her mind was racing faster than she had words to express it. Her first step was to race all the way to the roof of the building. Once she got to the top of the small apartment complex, she paused and considered how to escape.

Oh, right. I can just...

She put a particular plan into motion.

♂♀

Apartment building, Shinjuku

It was not a coincidence that Izaya Orihara was watching the TV at that exact moment.

Ikebukuro's 100-Day Front.

As an information broker, he was not likely to gain anything particularly fresh or juicy from this program, but given that it was an experiment in live broadcasting, he tuned in out of sheer curiosity, just in case something unexpected happened.

Namie had already gone back to her own apartment, and Izaya was enjoying some homemade French toast and basking in the glow of a recently completed major transaction.

"...Wow. Even I didn't see this coming."

What started as a live broadcast featuring Ikebukuro at night and a simple motorcycle waiting at a traffic light without a headlight suddenly shifted into a horror movie, then a stunning action blockbuster.

Celty turned her motorcycle into a horse, and a police bike chased after her.

"Suppose that cop is this Kinnosuke Kuzuhara I keep hearing about? His timing's either the best or the worst," he exclaimed, eyes narrowed, somewhere between laughter and exasperation. On the screen, the reporter was frantic.

"See that, folks? The mysterious figure riding what appeared to be a horse just used some strange means of climbing the wall to get onto the roof of the building! It seems the traffic patrol officer is calling for backup!"

"For better or for worse, Celty always managed to avoid my expectations for her," said Izaya Orihara, an information agent who made his base in Shinjuku.

He'd known Celty for years, he was aware of her dullahan identity, and he possessed a secret about her that even she didn't know.

That is, he possessed the head for which Celty had *formerly* been searching.

But for now, she didn't seem to be as fixated on the head, so he was keeping it secret just in case he could use it to achieve a desired outcome in the future.

"Oh dear. The problem is, modern society has decided that things like Celty don't exist. If she was the kind of alien you see in movies, the government and military would cover her existence up for her… but not in this case," Izaya cackled at the TV, talking to no one in particular.

Then something on the screen changed.

"Oh?"

"The rider in black is still silent up on the roof…ah! What is that?! Can you make it out through the camera?! The stars have vanished overhead! It's black! A large black curtain! Wh-whoa!"

The reporter's breathless commentary was accompanied by an odd object on the screen.

Something like enormous black wings that dimly reflected the city's lights leaped off the roof of the building and began a leisurely glide.

It was an enormous hang glider. In the center appeared to be a figure sitting atop a horse.

The problem was that the wings were far too huge for it. They spread

at least as wide as the building itself and nearly as big as a fighter jet, blocking out the stars.

For its tremendous size, the glider held no hint of mass or underlying structure. It slid effortlessly through the air, like a gigantic paper airplane. The flat, sky-spanning shadow caught a breeze passing between the buildings and began a low-altitude flight with a perfect view of Ikebukuro below.

"Damn! What do...think...are, Lupi...Third? Give up...face...justice! Oh, look at that! The traffic officer is chasing after her, shouting something! W-we're going to try to follow that flying object!"

The reporting team packed into their vehicle and roared their engine to follow the police bike. They didn't get far before the officer wheeled around and stuck it to the driver of the van.

"Hey! You're not an emergency vehicle, so you don't get to break the speed limit." "Oh? Y-yes, sir." "And obey the traffic lights." "Y-yes, sir!" "Uh, well, it looks like our driver is receiving instructions from the police officer, so let's send it back to the studio for a moment!"

The next instant, the feed cut, returning the picture to the stunned faces of the newscasters in the studio. Once they realized they were on camera, they turned to one another and began to deliver their opinions on what they'd seen.

Izaya had no interest in their thoughts. He slowly retrieved his cell phone from the recharging holster on the table and brought up a particular number.

♂♀

Several minutes earlier, apartment building, Ikebukuro

Two shadows writhed within the dark apartment room.

On the screen was the reality of Ikebukuro, happening right now.

The shadows huddled before the TV, conversing with bipolar intensities.

"...That's weird."

"It really is mysterious! Why, why, why? Why did the motorcycle turn into a horse? Why? That wasn't CG, right? It can't be! It's too cool for that! Isn't that crazy? It's like super-invincible-superman crazy! It's as crazy and mysterious as General Sherman or the titan arum!"

"...Be quiet."

"Oh, sorry, sorry! This part is important! But I can't stay quiet! Isn't this happening, like, just down the street? Let's go see it! C'mon! I don't think I can take this anymore! Oh, geez! I haven't been this excited since I saw the carnivorous giant cricket fight against the Goliath birdeater! I wanna see, I wanna see!"

The more excited shadow was cavorting around like a kid on a field trip bus ride, performing a rear naked choke hold on the other shadow. Even as the other shadow's face was going purple with the force of the fatal attack, it calmly raised its arm and pointed a small spray bottle at the shadow behind it.

"...Settle down."

The liquid within the bottle sprayed mercilessly on the other shadow's face.

"...?! Aaaaack!! I'm sorry, Kuru! I'll...I'll calm down...coff! Koff, hakk... Gahk... Please, not the habanero spray!" The excitable shadow writhed, coughing madly.

Only after flopping around and eventually landing in a break-dance rotation on its head did the afflicted shadow calm down.

"Ahh, that was really rough. You're so spartanical with your punishment, Kuru!" the shadow said, making up a word out of thin air. The girl she called Kuru ignored her and continued watching the TV.

"...Can't wait."

"Yeah, well, we only just started school! It's super-exciting to know we'll be spending the greatest moments of our youth in a city alongside something like *that*! Super-citing! Super-magic! Superbad!" she shouted inexplicably. Meanwhile, the immobile girl smiled as she watched the giant black wings on the screen.

While on the inside, her heart swirled with just as much desire as the other shadow.

♂♀

At that moment, Jack-o'-Lantern Japan Talent Agency Office, Higashi-Nakano

"Wowza! What? I mean, *what*? Holy hell in a handbasket!"

The effect of the pristine, ultraclean room with the pure white polished floor was broken by a very uncouth voice.

"I'll be damned if that ain't the most powerful image I ever seen! Now that's good stuff! In movie terms, that's got *Jurassic Park* impact! Or should it be *Godzilla*?"

An odd man was jabbering excitedly to himself in front of a television screen, his speech an oddly accented foreign take on Japanese. He had white skin and slicked-back blond hair, dark sunglasses and facial stubble, a white suit and crocodile-skin bag, expensive rings and a thick cigar in his mouth—the Hollywood image of a fat-cat villain if there ever was one.

The screen in front of him was too big for most people to consider a "television." It was a good one hundred inches in measurement, the kind of screen most people could only dream of affording.

The interior was a modern office building of the type one would expect to see in some American tech company, with each desk in its own fully screened cubicle that afforded the employee inside a small manner of personal office space.

But the space that housed this noisy man and his giant TV was placed separately, with a wide-open floor plan and several couches and tables, a kind of pseudo–conference room set up for viewing the massive screen in the back.

It was an odd office design that held many personal spaces and a lobby in the same large room. The man was excitedly fixed on the screen.

"Wish I could just zip on over to Ikebukuro right now! Hot damn, I do! Yeah! Hey, what's Mr. Yuuhei doin' today? He knows Ikebukuro—he can show us around the town! We'll get a real good look at that Sleepy Hollow business as we enjoy some traditional flower viewing!" he chattered, his eyes sparkling like a child's. Meanwhile, the more rational men seated around the TV exchanged concerned murmurs with each other.

"A stunt by Daioh?" "No, that's not their demographic." "Gotta call the producer..." "Anyone out on assignment in the area right now?" "I can call the manager in the studio..."

While the Japanese men took the abnormal situation on the screen with tense consternation, the white man shook his head and held up his hands in complaint.

"Hey! Hey, hey, hey! You ignoring *my* opinion? *The boss?*"

"Boss, we can't see the screen."

"Oh, whoops… Sorry about that. Wait, that ain't the point! Why am I treated like the odd man out? Or is this a racist thing? You don't wanna work for a foreigner! I thought Japan was a land that cherished harmony, huh? Are you givin' your own country a bad name?"

"Maybe you should stop giving your *own* country a bad name, boss… Also, you're the one disrupting the harmony. Especially when Yuuhei's film is doing such good business," said one of his employees. The company president shrugged and looked away.

The man's name was Max Sandshelt.

He was the president of the Japanese branch of the American-based talent agency Jack-o'-Lantern. The agency was a big-time player with connections to the McDonnell Company, a major movie distributor, but in Japan they were mid-tier at best. Compared to the big boys, they had an unbalanced stable of talent, with a few top-class actors and a majority of unremarkable youngsters.

At a glance, he looked incompetent, but for whatever reason, his ability to produce talent, forge connections, and escape trouble at the last possible moment were nothing short of genius, which earned him enough regard to function as the company president.

Of course, the reason he needed to get out of trouble at the last possible moment was almost always his own fault.

"Dammit all, the only ones on my side are the sweet little things I helped turn into works of art. The only ones who will eternally understand my soul are the angels that bring happiness to the world," he slurred sadly.

A prim secretarial woman respectfully said, "Please do your job, boss. Also, we just did our flower viewing last week, and Yuuhei Hanejima went back to his home in Ikebukuro after filming today. Also, why is your English so shaky, if you originally came from America?"

"Oh, brother, whatta buncha sticks-in-the-mud you are. See, the times demand real impact, somethin' new and never before seen. That's why I want a glimpse of that Headless Rider… Ah! Eureka!" the president jabbered, completely ignoring his secretary. He excitedly dialed a number, humming to himself.

Great, another harebrained scheme!

Every employee present grumbled restlessly at the sight of the boss's sparkling gaze and resumed their conversations, only the content had entirely changed to complaints about their employer.

♂♀

At that moment, Ikebukuro

As the police motorcycle's engine roared off into the distance, Celty heard the sudden eruption of her phone from the spot where she was hidden.

It nearly scared her witless when it happened, but once she was satisfied that there were no police officers around, she hesitantly accepted the call and pressed the phone to her ear.

"Ah, finally got through... Hey, Celty. Sounds like you're in trouble."

Izaya!

She wondered what would cause the information dealer to call her at this particular time. And the way he opened the call suggested to her that he realized what was happening to her.

"Wondering how I know what's happening to you right now? Don't worry. I don't have you bugged or anything. Besides, Shinra would spot something like that right away. He's so desperate to hog you all to himself, he wouldn't dare allow anyone to pry into your home privacy."

I'm going to go sock this idiot a good one and thank Shinra later.

Celty kept the cell phone pressed to her helmet, imagining that a vein was bulging on her nonexistent head. She and Izaya usually discussed business through text messages, but there were times that he called her so that he could speak uninterrupted.

She decided to keep the line open, knowing that he wouldn't just call for no good reason.

"That was a clever idea, I have to say, creating a *fake version* of yourself and your bike out of shadow to put on the glider."

"..."

She felt a clenching at her heart. *Is he watching from somewhere after all?*

Izaya was correct—she had instantly created black models of herself and her trusty steed from that special solid shadow of hers, then sent the whole thing gliding through the air to distract her foes.

Was it actually really obvious?

Celty was still on top of the roof, waiting a few seconds for the cop and TV crew to chase after the decoy so she could slip away in the opposite direction. While she was shocked that Izaya had seen through this ruse, it also made her worry that the police officer could figure it out just as easily.

Izaya laughed as if he could read her mind and said, "Oh, don't worry. They'd have to know you really well to see through that fake. But I didn't see the colored helmet, and you know that there's no escaping the motorcycle cop at the speed that thing's gliding."

Well, he's perfectly correct, but hearing him explain it so confidently is kind of irritating. Did he call me just to brag about his deductions?

So much for her assumption that he wouldn't call for frivolous reasons. Celty lowered the phone to stop the call. But through her heightened sense of hearing, she still heard his voice loud and clear.

"Well, starting tomorrow things are going to get kind of crazy, so I thought I'd give you a heads-up."

?

She waited for the answer, curious. On the other end, Izaya made a request.

"Until things calm down, *absolutely* do not come to my office. I'll send you an e-mail with the details, but I didn't want you showing up before you could see it."

Huh? Celty wanted to ask him what he meant, but given that it was just an audio call without text functionality, there was no way for her to convey her thoughts to him.

"Well, so long. Best of luck."

"Best of luck?"

He hung up the phone call, without her expressing a single thing on her mind.

What's up with him?

Completely bewildered, Celty decided that escaping the roof was her top priority at the moment and stashed away her phone. But that left her with a strong feeling of *wrongness*.

Her shadow-made riding suit had a chest pocket for storing things. In normal circumstances, it didn't hold anything other than her cell phone. But at this particular point in time, it wasn't right for it to be empty.

She reached for her other chest pocket, feeling something cold stealing over her back. The other pocket held only her PDA, and her waist pocket had nothing but her apartment key, just like always.

It was all of her normal belongings.

Which meant that the one extra item she was carrying around today was not in her possession.

The plain brown envelope with "Payment—Celty Sturluson" written on it.

She fell to her knees in shock, realizing the unavoidable truth.

I lost the envelope full of my pay.
I dropped my envelope…of one million yen!

She looked around desperately, but the bag was not on the roof with her. Most likely, it had fallen loose while she was riding away from the motorcycle cop. But she had been so desperate and panicked in the moment that she couldn't remember which route she'd taken.

The Coiste Bodhar, in its original horse form, nuzzled closer to comfort its owner, but the severed end of its neck merely bumped against her helmet. It created the illusion of two headless creatures fighting over which could use the helmet as a head.

Celty's night passed quietly, locked in that comical pose.

Without realizing what effect her actions would have upon the city.

Without realizing the twists of fate that the envelope she dropped would bring about.

The headless knight, locked in modern times, mourned for a very human reason.

Chat room

Kanra: Heeeere's Kanra!
TarouTanaka: Hello.
Bacura: 'Sup.
Saika: good evening. it is a pleasure again today.
Kanra: Sure thing. ☆ Is everyone used to the new chat system by now?
TarouTanaka: Yes, the different colors for each person makes it easy to identify who's who.
Bacura: Indeed,
Bacura: This allows us to gang up on Kanra more vividly than ever.
Kanra: Vividly?! Oh no, what are you going to do to little old me?!
Bacura: An endless repetition of beatings and neglect.
Kanra: This is more than bullying. It sounds just like a group lynching!
Bacura: Uh, exactly?
TarouTanaka: Lol, that's so messed up, Bacura.
Saika: cant we all just get along
Bacura: Er, actually,
Bacura: Saika,
Bacura: I don't truly hate Kanra in reality.

<Private Mode> Kanra: You're such a liar. You hate me with every fiber of your being.
<Private Mode> Bacura: Shut up and die.

Kanra: That's right! This is how we get along! He's a *tsundere*, he hates the things he loves.
Bacura: I'd say my ratio is more like *tsun-tsun-dere-tsun, dere-tsun-tsun-tsun-tsun-tsun-tsun-die*.
Kanra: What kind of *tsun-to-dere* ratio is that?!
Bacura: It was a song that the children at the Sakurashinmachi shopping district were singing.
Kanra: And it ended with "die"?!
Bacura: No, that was my own twist on it. Why?
Kanra: That's awful!
TarouTanaka: It really is, lol.

*   *   *

Setton has entered the chat.

Setton: Evening...
TarouTanaka: Oh, good evening.
Setton: I can't take it any more.
Kanra: Good evening. ☆
Bacura: Evenin'.
TarouTanaka: What's the matter?
Saika: good evening, it is nice to see you
Setton: Unfortunately, I lost some money...
Bacura: ?!
TarouTanaka: Oh, that's terrible... Did you tell the police about it?
Setton: No.
Setton: Er, sorry, I mean, yes. I did.
Kanra: Ooh, how much did you lose?
Setton: Actually, it was the envelope with my entire salary for the month...
Saika: are you all right
Bacura: ?!
TarouTanaka: Why, that's terrible! Is everything okay?!
Setton: Yes, I've got enough savings that it won't affect my budget, but it's a bummer...
Kanra: Cheer up!
Kanra: As a matter of fact, I have good news for you, Setton!
Setton: What's that?
Kanra: Heh-heh! Check out <u>this</u> address!
TarouTanaka: Ooh, you can paste links to text now?
Bacura: Cool.

<Private Mode> TarouTanaka: What is this, Izaya?!

Saika: um, what does this mean

<Private Mode> TarouTanaka: Why does this say there's a bounty on Celty's head?!

Setton: Oh, this is beyond my ability. I could never catch the Black Rider.

* * *

\<Private Mode\> Kanra: Remember how Celty was all on camera during that live program?

\<Private Mode\> Kanra: Well, some film production company put out a bounty on anyone who can identify her. Apparently they want to develop her for show business...

\<Private Mode\> TarouTanaka: That's completely irrational!

\<Private Mode\> Kanra: Well, Celty's very existence is kind of irrational.

Bacura: Ten million yen?

Bacura: Isn't that crazy?

Saika: im sorry, i have to go for tonight

Setton: Oh, I need to take a bath, so I've got to go for now.

TarouTanaka: Oh, good night.

Kanra: Good niiight! ☆

Setton: Night.

Saika: good night, thank you

Setton has left the chat.
Saika has left the chat.

Bacura: Good nighters.

Bacura: Whoops, too late.

Kanra: Shall we log off too? We can talk about that bounty next time.

Kanra: Well, good night! ☆

TarouTanaka: Good night.

Bacura: (>_<)ノ ゞ

Kanra has left the chat.
TarouTanaka has left the chat.
Bacura has left the chat.

The chat room is currently empty.

.

.

.

Next morning, near Kawagoe Highway, top floor of apartment building

"I'm home. Wow, what a terrible day."

The luxury apartment was larger than your average one-story home.

Shinra Kishitani, the owner of this extravagant living space—which boasted five rooms in addition to the kitchen and over 1,600 square feet—returned home in his extremely recognizable white lab coat to see his loving partner.

"Uh, where are you, Celty? I'm so, so exhausted. I got wrapped up in this very strange business. You've heard about being the one 'left holding the bag'? Well, I just got stuck with one of the biggest bags of all time, and… Celty? Celty? What's the matter? …Are you home? She said the session would be over by the evening…"

He walked down the hallway curiously, then noticed that something in the apartment was wrong.

Despite all of the lights being on, the living room was oddly dark.

"?"

He trotted over and spotted a black cocoon in the corner of the room.

"Wha—?!"

Celty had fashioned herself a huge cocoon out of her own shadow, like some kind of gigantic silkworm. Sensing that she was inside of it, Shinra forgot his fatigue and leaped onto the shadow.

The cocoon immediately cracked open and swallowed Shinra's body like a carnivorous plant.

"Whoa…hey!"

Shocked and bewildered by his unexpected entrance to the cocoon, Shinra found it to be a world of pleasure.

As he imagined, Celty was inside the cocoon. She clutched him tight. It was dark inside, so he couldn't see, but he recognized the familiar feeling of her body.

"Wha…?! They say, 'Time and tide wait for no man,' but I feel like my sense of reason is crumbling and putting me 'on cloud nine,' and… uh…what…?" he babbled flippantly in his usual way but quickly came to his senses when he noticed that Celty's actions were uncharacteristically stiff.

Suddenly, a light blinded him. He figured out that it was Celty's PDA screen and narrowed his eyes until he could read the letters.

"*Sorry. Just stay with me for a bit.*"

"Actually, I would be perfectly delighted to…but what's the matter, Celty? You seem rather upset."

"*I'm not rather upset. I'm inconsolably upset. So console me.*"

"You are the most depressed dominatrix I've ever seen."

Relieved that at least she wasn't openly discussing suicide, Shinra held her gently and decided to hear her out.

"…So you lost a million yen and then earned yourself a bounty ten times that amount?"

"*Yes, so now I can't just ride around outside. It would be very bad if people found out I was here.*"

Relatively relieved after getting her troubles off her chest, Celty released her cocoon at last. Shinra was a bit disappointed that their private haven was gone, but he was wise enough not to comment on it.

He continued to console her, offering her a reassuring smile. "Just relax, Celty. The apartment building has tremendous security, and we can choose to believe that one way or another, that money will find its way back into your hands. As they say, 'Sadness and gladness succeed each other.'"

"*Yes…but I'm sorry, I really am.*"

"Why are you apologizing to me?"

"*I was going to buy some electronics with that money. And…well, I was going to buy you a present of some kind, but so much for that. It's all gone. Sorry. Oh, I wasn't saying that to demand gratitude from you… I don't know. Just forget I said it.*"

She folded up the PDA and bashfully looked away. This gesture pierced Shinra directly through the heart, and he embraced her again.

"Celty! You're the bes— *Mfgfgfg!*"

"*Thank you, Shinra. But don't get carried away, because I'm not in the mood.*"

She pulled away from him right as he attempted to fondle her breast, leaving Shinra alone in the middle of the shadow cocoon. Unperturbed, he happily announced, "Ha-ha-ha, I'll be waiting for the moment when you *are* in the mood."

"*So will I.*"

She pulled his head out of the cocoon so he could see the PDA, and his face lit up with youthful delight. As if prompted by the moment, Celty's cell phone rang. It was a text message, which she read, then picked up her helmet off the table.

"I've got work. I'll be right back."

"Are you sure? Maybe you should stay back and lie low for today…"

"Trust is the biggest element of a courier's work. Don't worry, I won't cause trouble for you."

"Oh, you can give me trouble. We're family; you can make all the trouble you want," Shinra said. His smile caused her heart to leap momentarily. Regretting that she had no smile to return to him, she awkwardly attempted an emoticon on her PDA.

"Thanks. (^^)⌐ "

Shinra's waiting for me at home. That's enough to give me the strength of a hundred.

She left the apartment with confident strides, feeling power course through her.

"Well, that seems to have cheered you up. I'm glad."

All that she left behind was a solitary man, wrapped up inside a black cocoon with his head poking out.

"Huh…? Wait, Celty, I don't think I can get out of this shadow cocoon. Hey, Celty? Hello? Hey, I can't get out of here!"

♂♀

Half a day later, Ikebukuro

Yes, Shinra's waiting for me at home. That's enough to give me the strength of a hundred.

Celty raced along on her bike, recalling her bold determination early that morning.

But…I don't know if I can get home through this…

All around her was engine roaring and horn blaring.

She concentrated her senses in all directions without turning around. She could sense at least twenty around her.

The men straddled specially modified motorcycles and wore special gang uniforms with striped patterns. Their vehicles were triple seated with amplifying mufflers, gaudy stickers, and various options that did not seem at all necessary.

Nearly all of them were modified to fall into the category of "gang bikes," flashy and obnoxious—which meant that, needless to say, this was an honest-to-god motorcycle gang.

"*Uraaah!* I said stop the bike!"

"You want us ta run you off the road? Huh?!"

"*Uhyo-rrra!* Tah! Tah! Dahh!"

A two-man bike that stuck close to Celty swung over, the man in the rear seat waving metal pipes at her.

Oh man, I didn't know there were still people this stereotypical in forward-thinking Tokyo!

Of course, Celty herself was not exactly normal in appearance. She was dressed in her usual style, but she had fashioned a pitch-black sidecar to carry her payload.

Sitting in the seat was a black container about the size of a large golf bag, attached to the Coiste Bodhar via the temporary sidecar, which was made out of Celty's shadow. The long bag was seated upright in the car.

Celty didn't know what was inside of it, but based on the size and shape…she was very certain that she didn't want to try to imagine too hard.

About thirty minutes earlier, Celty was reading a tabloid on a bench, waiting for her client to finish her afternoon job.

Wow, Shizuo's brother is getting into mischief.

There was a massive headline on the front page reading "Yuuhei Hanejima and Ruri Hijiribe in a Late-Night Tryst?!" accompanied by an article that didn't add much more to that. Two of the biggest young stars in the nation were caught meeting secretly at night.

And they were spotted right outside of Yuuhei Hanejima's apartment at that.

Even though it had happened right there in Ikebukuro as well, the article about Celty from last night wasn't even top billing. Society seemed to have more interest in the practical romance of a man and woman than in some unidentified monster.

Ruri Hijiribe? Who would have thought?

Ruri Hijiribe was one of the hottest pop idols in the nation and had rocketed to the top of everyone's attention a few years ago, through participating in a variety of media.

They sold her as a reserved, laid-back, and slightly weak-willed character, and despite being fully Japanese, there was a kind of Scandinavian beauty to her features, to the extent that even Celty couldn't deny that she found the girl very cute.

Both Yuuhei and Ruri were adults over twenty but looked younger than their real age. So a passionate affair between the two held an irresistible romantic sway—at least, judging by the way the papers were trying to depict it.

Before she could read further into the article, her client appeared, and she took off with the payload as instructed.

She hadn't been set upon by the cameramen or police officers she expected. The morning job concluded without trouble, and things went so smoothly that it was almost a letdown after all of her fearful anticipation.

However...

Just when she was ready to feel relief, she ran into the obnoxious motorcycle gang on the main road. At first she was confused, but when she heard the cries of "That's our ten million yen right there!" she remembered her current plight.

Before she even had time to sigh, the neighborhood of Ikebukuro became the setting for a spectacular car chase.

"Raaah!"

"Don't mess with Toramaru, sucker!"

The men on motorcycles, decorated with gang stickers bearing a name that seemed to remind her of a manga title, swung their weapons wildly. The average age of motorcycle gangs was rising, she'd heard, and sure enough, all of these men appeared to be in their twenties from what she could see.

Damn... Shouldn't you be old enough to have grown out of this bounty-hunting nonsense? And isn't Toramaru a gang from Saitama?

What are they doing here?! This must be the power of a hefty bounty at work!

Ten million yen was indeed a preposterous reward just for capturing Celty. So much that even she was considering turning herself in to gain the money. It was only the sinking feeling that it would not be worth it in the long run that convinced her to ignore the bounty.

On the other hand, that didn't stop other people from coming after her. There were flags from other teams aside from Toramaru in the mix now.

"Th' hell you doin'?!"

"Fuck off! That Black Rider's ours, dammit!"

"Don't mess with the Pylori Kings!"

"We'll give you chronic gastritis, bitch!"

Celty decided to pick up her pace while the gangs turned on one another.

Aw, crap. I could just fight all of them off...but that'll only make the situation worse for Shinra, and I don't want that. I should try to get away for now and ask someone for advice. But who do you go to for trouble like this...?

Just then, one of the bikers she was about to leave in the dust swung his metal pipe wildly. "You ain't goin' nowhere!"

The tip of the pipe ripped through the edge of the bag holding Celty's payload.

A human arm rolled out of the tear.

...

" " " " " " " " " "
... ...

Celty and all of the gang members around her fell silent as a group.

Ah yes. As I feared. I had a feeling this was the case. I should have known! Celty thought, squeezing her helmet on tight and holding back tears.

The other riders followed along in silence, not sure how to react. In that empty space, a single voice could be heard.

"Oh, this isn't good. This is very bad news for you."

It was a voice she'd heard only a few times before. But Celty knew whom that voice belonged to. It was engraved into her soul.

"This is more than just traffic violations we're talking about now."

It can't be.

It can't be, it can't be, it can't be.

You're kidding! Not now! You can't do this to me now!

She looked over, not praying as much as cursing the rest of the world—and witnessed her worst fears come to life.

At some point, a police officer on his white motorcycle had cut through the gangs to pull up alongside her.

"I'll give you one warning... Pull your bike over to the left shoulder."

Whaaaaaaaaaaaaaaa—?!

Celty's entire body burst with shadows, which she tried to use as a smoke screen to escape. But the cop made his way through them somehow, staying tight to her side.

"I told you...traffic cops aren't gonna back down from a little show like that!"

No, that's just you!

The bikers pulled back to a safer distance, startled by her shadows, but her mortal enemy, the determined traffic cop, steadily closed, not intimidated in the least by her monstrous form.

"Goddammit! Stay outta this, pig! Shit!" one of the bikers yelled, swinging his pipe closer. The officer easily evaded the blow—

And Celty pretended not to see what happened next.

I didn't see that, didn't see that. Didn't see anything.

The officer pushed the parallel gangster's bike over until the driver's face was nearly scraping the asphalt, holding it in place for nearly five seconds before pulling him back upright.

Celty did witness the absolutely irrational action but spontaneously decided that it was in her best interest to immediately forget about it before she contemplated what it meant for her.

I didn't see that! I didn't see anything!

The biker slowly coasted to a stop, drool dripping from his mouth, his eyes empty. The other bikers watched the entire display in disbelieving silence but only for a moment.

"Wh...wha...what the hell you think you're doin', cop?!"

"Kill him!"

The biker gang switched targets to the officer on his white motorcycle and promptly surrounded him.

What ensued was a battle at sixty miles per hour.

Vehicles racing between the law-abiding traffic, separated into the prey and the pursuer, and the one who intended to arrest them both.

Celty took advantage of the conflict between the cop and the bikers to slip down a side street. But all she found there was yet another biker gang.

Am I really going to make it home today?

She spun her motorcycle around and raced back to the main street to avoid the new gang of twenty-strong bikers. That only succeeded in adding yet another large group to the absurd chase.

She heard a chopper noise overhead.

The Headless Rider raced through the evening light, wondering if even the helicopter above was chasing after her. If she had a face, it would be tear streaked by now. Celty envisioned the face of her love—and then remembered something.

She hadn't dissolved the shadow cocoon that Shinra was trapped inside.

Oh, Shinra. I'm sorry.

If I don't make it home…I'm so sorry!

As for the target of that message, Shinra was up on the top floor of the apartment building, lying on the floor of the living room, grinning happily and staring vaguely into nothing as he talked to himself.

"Ohhh… Is this one of those kinky abandonment things?"

CHAPTER 2
YOUTH MAGAZINE MAO
**"NEW SPRING LIFE! HIGH
SCHOOLERS' TOKYO DEBUT SPECIAL!
IKEBUKURO EDITION"**

"Everything gets refreshed in the spring!

A new life and new encounters in a new town!

Have you found new people since your move to Ikebukuro?

If you have, leap up to the next step by following this guide to enhance your Ikebukuro life and meet the perfect partner!"

♂♀

The boy skimmed through the article, then promptly took the magazine to the register.

His name was Mikado Ryuugamine.

He was a student entering his second year at Raira Academy, a private school in the heart of Ikebukuro. It was his second year in Ikebukuro, but for some reason, he was searching for articles about starting a new life in the neighborhood. There were already three such magazines in his bag.

The boy left the convenience store and headed right into the karaoke place next door. It was well known for serving restaurant-quality food and having an ample selection of songs available to sing.

Mikado walked inside, looking nervous, and told the employee at the desk that he was meeting someone, then gave the room number.

In a large room on the sixth floor, he found that several people were already waiting inside.

"Yoo-hoo! How you been, Mika-poo?"

"You're late. We already ordered a big ol' pitcher of oolong tea!"

The first two to speak were a boy and girl in casual, stylish outfits. They looked as sharp as fashion models, but that image was ruined by the mountains of manga, books, games, anime DVDs, and merchandise stacked around them.

Next to them was a blushing girl wearing the same uniform as Mikado, holding a figurine of a girl wearing a scandalously revealing outfit. When she noticed that he was there, she shrieked and quickly returned the figurine to Karisawa.

"Uh, err...may I sit next to you, Sonohara?"

"...Um, yes!" the quiet girl with the glasses said, her face red. In truth, her own proportions were worthy of the figurine's. "W-welcome, Mikado."

"Sorry about showing up late. Sorry to you, too, Karisawa and Yumasaki," Mikado said, dipping his head. The other boy and girl smiled kindly.

"It's okay. We've got plenty of time around midday."

"That's right. Essentially, we're free to hang out during the business hours of any bookstore."

Unlike the relaxed street-clothes duo, the uniformed couple was awkward. An employee came into the room to take a drink order, the door shut, and then they were ready to get down to business.

"So, what did you want to ask us?"

"Well...I feel awkward even having to ask...," Mikado began, sighing heavily and looking for the right words before continuing.

"Can you...teach us how to guide someone around Ikebukuro?"

♂♀

Two hours earlier

Raira Academy was brimming with new students after its official entrance ceremony.

Mikado and Anri were in the same class again and voted to be the representatives for the second year running. After they attended a brief meeting with the other student body representatives, Mikado was hurrying to catch up to Anri when he was stopped from behind.

"Um, excuse me! Are you Mr. Ryuugamine?"

He turned around to see a boy wearing the Raira Academy uniform.

"Uh, and you are... Let's see, we just had introductions. Aoba?"

"Yes! Aoba Kuronuma, first-year student!"

The sparkling-eyed boy had a girlish face and short stature, which made him look like a middle schooler at a glance, if not outright elementary school. Mikado knew that he himself skewed young in appearance, but the boy here had him beat in that regard by a mile.

"I was so surprised to overhear you introducing yourself! It's really you!" the boy chattered excitedly, but Mikado was confused.

Who is this? Have I met him somewhere before?

If that was the case, it would be rude to have forgotten his face, even if he was a lower-ranking student. Mikado's face scrunched up as he tried to remember, but nothing was coming to mind.

The boy named Aoba Kuronuma recognized the troubled look on his face and smiled gently. "Oh, I'm sorry. Don't worry. It's our first meeting. I only just learned your name a minute ago!"

"Oh, I see. Wait...why were you so surprised, then?" Mikado asked, a perfectly reasonable question. The boy's eyes lit up with excitement.

"Because...oh." He shut his mouth for a moment, looked around cautiously, then whispered.

"Aren't you...*in the Dollars?*"

"...!"

Mikado's eyes went wide, and his mouth worked soundlessly.

"Wh-what do you mean?" he finally squeaked, just as he heard the vibrating of his cell phone from within his schoolbag. Based on the length of the sound, it had to be an e-mail.

"Oh, you finally got it," the boy said, grinning.

Mikado hastily pulled his phone out and saw a message from the Dollars' mailing list. It was a message to all from one of the hundreds of people on the mailing list that read, *"I'm recruiting new members from Raira Academy! Please tell me how it's going at other schools!"*

Mikado noticed the username "Wakaba Mark" and looked back at the other boy.

"Wait, are you saying...?"

"Yes, I'm Wakaba Mark! I was just about the six hundredth person to join the Dollars, but you remember how the registration site got trashed and went down? So my name's not in there anymore..."

"H-how did you know I was one of the Dollars?" the older boy asked, clearly rattled, while the younger just showed off a cheeky, confident smirk.

"I didn't know for sure. But...remember when we had that Dollars meetup in real life a year ago? You were there in the middle, talking to that woman who was our target, right? The image just stuck in my head ever since!"

The Dollars were a unique organization that increased its power through the Internet.

They were ostensibly categorized as a color-based street gang, but the ties that bound the group together were loose at best, yet extremely wide ranging. They had been in a state of conflict with another gang called the Yellow Scarves until recently, when the hostilities abruptly cooled, and now both sides were keeping calm.

If the Dollars were a color gang, the color they repped was either "colorless" or "camouflage." They blended into the town with alarming ease, never gathering with a unified color to announce their presence.

They were connected through cell phones and the Internet—hidden bonds that rarely took physical form in modern society.

The teenage girls or housewives you passed on the street could be Dollars. The ability to plant that seed of doubt was the Dollars' shield. And the possibility that it was true was the Dollars' sword.

The Dollars were a gang with an eerie form of expansion. Their founder was shrouded in mystery, and almost none of its members knew who the leader was.

And at this precise moment, the very founder and source of that mystery was sweating buckets at some uncomfortable questions from a new kid at school.

*　　*　　*

"Umm, uhh, you don't have the wrong idea, do you?"

"You got that e-mail."

"Ah, ahhh. G-good point."

"So you *do* keep it hidden! Don't worry. I can keep a secret! I'm very good at protecting others' secrets, in fact!" Aoba said, his eyes shining with reverence. Mikado was frozen still, completely at a loss for how to respond.

In fact, Mikado had found himself in trouble a year ago, when a huge company was—

"But what was so special about that night? Mr. Ryuugamine, are you actually an officer of the Dollars or something?"

"No, no, no! The Dollars don't have those! I-I'm just an errand runner, that's all!"

"Oh, really? Well, anyway, I'm just excited to know that someone from the Dollars is so close nearby!"

His childlike impression extended to his actions, not just his looks. From a distance they looked like middle school brothers, but they were both fully fledged high schoolers.

Mikado wavered on how to respond, then gave up and, with a careful look around, told his younger schoolmate, "All right. But you shouldn't talk about it at school, and I'd appreciate it if you kept this as secret as possible."

The words were cold and distant, but Aoba's face broke into a delighted beam. "Sure thing! But I have one request of you…"

"Request?"

"I don't really know much about Ikebukuro. So can you show me around the city?"

♂♀

He conferred with Anri after that but still didn't feel confident in his ability to give a tour, so he resignedly turned to people he knew who were more knowledgeable about the area—and that turned out to be Yumasaki and Karisawa.

Man, if Masaomi were still here, I wouldn't have to go through all this trouble, Mikado grumbled to himself, then banished the thought.

Masaomi Kida was a longtime friend of Mikado's who had vanished on him and Anri. As a major figure of the Yellow Scarves, who were feuding with the Dollars, he decided he needed to get out of town after they learned each other's secrets. It didn't really matter to Mikado, but Masaomi had his own thoughts about the ordeal, and Mikado wasn't going to pry.

Don't even start. If you can't handle this without relying on Masaomi, then you can't hold your head up and smile when he comes back.

Mikado waited for Masaomi's return for his own reasons. Praying that on the day the three of them came together, they could laugh and smile again.

"Mikado! Mikado, what's up? Hellooo?"

"Huh?!" he said, snapping back to attention as he heard his name.

"Are you sleepy? Should we give you a wake-up call with some anime songs?"

"Uh, er, aaah! S-sorry!" Mikado stammered, back to reality after his long contemplation of Masaomi and the Yellow Scarves.

When they got down to the details, Yumasaki and Karisawa were more gung ho on the idea than he expected. They began to argue among themselves about which spots were best to show a young man around Ikebukuro.

At first, the pair was recommending Animate, Toranoana, Yellow Submarine, and other hard-core nerd spots, but Mikado was relieved that they eventually settled into more mainstream, recognizable names.

Suddenly, Karisawa looked up at Mikado and suggested, "Why don't we just go with you?"

"Huh?"

"You're not going to have much time to learn detailed info about the places we're listing off for you. So shouldn't we just go with you? Plus, we don't know what this younger kid is like. It might be best to make adjustments to the plan on the fly after we meet him in person."

"Well..."

Mikado wasn't sure how to respond. It would be a huge help, of course, but he didn't know what kind of impression they would leave on a relatively normal schoolmate. They *looked* normal, sure, but all they had to do was open their mouths to reveal their status as ambassadors from the 2-D realm. What's worse, they had no intention of meeting people halfway in that regard.

It didn't bother Mikado that much, but what would Aoba Kuronuma think?

Well, they're approachable, and they're pretty nice. It shouldn't be a problem, Mikado thought, an eternal optimist who blindly believed in the concept that if you just talked to someone, you could find common understanding.

"Are you sure you'd be up for that?"

"Oh, sure thing. We're free this evening, anyway."

"It's not going to create a work conflict or anything?" Mikado asked in concern, but Karisawa just looked nonplussed.

"Oh? We didn't tell you?"

"?"

"Yumacchi and I are freelancers, so we can make our own schedules."

"Freelancers...?" Mikado asked curiously.

Karisawa took a sip of oolong tea and continued, "That's right. Dotachin's more of an artisan type. And Togusacchi lives off the rent from the apartment building that he and his brother inherited from their parents. His brother manages the place, while Togusacchi collects the rent money. The reason we can hang out with them so much is because we set our own hours. Of course, until a year ago, everyone except for Dotachin was unemployed."

Now that she mentioned it, Mikado could tell that they weren't salaried office types, given that they were meeting him in the middle of a weekday like this. And when he saw them around town, they were always hanging around in their own clothes, no uniforms. They were often with Kadota's group, but he had to admit that he just assumed the whole bunch had no jobs.

"I make money by selling engraved accessories on the Net, and would you believe what Yumacchi does? What is it, ice sculpting? People pay him to make those ice sculptures you see at parties and stuff."

"Whoa!"

"Actually, I'm not even that great. I don't have exclusive arrangements with a hotel or anything reliable like that, so I never know when my income will dry up. But the character sculptures I've done for publishers' parties lately have been a big hit, so if I can survive on that, it's my dream job. Wanna be the next Kaiyodo." Yumasaki smiled shyly, referencing a famous figurine maker.

Mikado murmured in surprise, impressed that the two had actual jobs. Based on how wide Anri's eyes were, he wasn't the only one who assumed they were unemployed. Given the piles of books they seemed to be buying every single day, that income was pretty sizable. Of course, knowing them, they were probably cutting into their food budgets to squeeze in more books.

He bowed to the pair. "In that case, I'd be delighted to have your help! Hope to see you tomorrow!"

But when Yumasaki followed that up with, "In that case, we'll start off with a pilgrimage of all the holy sites of Ikebukuro that appear in anime and manga," Mikado's gratitude quickly plummeted into regret.

♂♀

Two hours later, Ikebukuro West Gate Park

"We'll pay the bill. Just let us sing," Karisawa had said. Mikado and Anri reluctantly agreed and were treated to a two-hour medley of anime theme songs for their trouble.

They hardly recognized any of them, but Karisawa and Yumasaki were surprisingly talented singers and as comfortable as if they'd practiced singing hundreds of times. In fact, it was probably true that they had practiced the same *song* hundreds of times before.

They especially seemed to like a recent anime theme sung by a pop idol named Ruri Hijiribe—both Yumasaki and Karisawa chose it on different occasions.

After the karaoke was done and they left the singers behind, Mikado and Anri were walking through West Gate Park, chatting.

"Thanks for coming with me today."

"Oh, it's fine. I needed to thank them, anyway..."

"You did? For what?"

"For some stuff a while ago...," Anri said vaguely. Mikado didn't want to intrude, so he searched for a new topic. He was going to ask her if anything interesting had happened to her over spring vacation when something odd caught his eye.

It was a white gas mask.

In a corner of West Gate Park was a man wearing the strange combination of a white gas mask and lab coat, speaking with a tall Caucasian fellow.

Mikado didn't want to stare, so he kept tabs on the man out of the side of his eye as he noted, "I wonder what that guy in the white gas mask is all about... The foreigner next to him isn't wearing one, so it can't be a gas leak..."

But Anri didn't respond.

He looked over in case she hadn't heard him and instantly noticed that something was wrong with her. Anri was looking in the same direction that he had just been doing, but her eyes were wide with shock.

"Um, Sonohara...?"

"Oh...sorry. I was just thinking, that white gas mask is very strange..."

"Huh? Uh, yeah. Yeah, it sure is," Mikado remarked, glad that Anri was back to her usual smile, before he headed for home.

Meanwhile, Anri started on the route to her apartment—but once she checked to make sure that Mikado was completely out of sight, she returned the way they had come.

♂♀

"Well, if you want to know more...shall we find a more private place to talk?"

"The details are in the data you gave me, aren't they? No use for idle chat."

"I think you'd be better off hearing me out. Don't want you to examine the data and assume it's just a joke."

"What do you mean?"

The two men were keeping their expressions hidden, albeit in different ways.

The large white man was utterly stone-faced.

And the Japanese man was hiding his entire face behind a gas mask.

Anri carefully approached the tense, uncomfortable scene. Instantly, the white man sensed her and turned around, looking down with a gentle smile.

"Did you want something, sweet little girl?" he said in perfect Japanese, despite his obviously foreign origin. Anri tensed instinctually, sensing something dangerous from him. But running away now would defeat the purpose, so she bowed to him and then turned to the man in the gas mask.

"Um…thank you…for the other day," she said, then belatedly regretted it, as she didn't even know his name. Still, she could clearly remember the day last month when she was talking with Celty, and the same man had butted in to ask, *Are you the daughter of the Sonohara-dou?*

Given his outfit, it would be hard to mistake him for anyone else. She bowed again, and he seemed to recognize her at last. The man in the gas mask glanced at the white man and said, "As long as it's brief," then turned back to her.

"You're the girl from the Sonohara-dou. I'm afraid I left quite a miserable impression on you back then."

"Um…do you know my parents?"

"Well, I should say that yes, I do. And on an extension of that, I also know about the *sword you possess.*"

"…!"

Instantly, a voice ran through Anri's right arm.

A voice that only she could hear, going straight to her brain.

Ooh. If it isn't my former owner.

That voice, which belonged to a plane distinct from physics or psychology, was not the "cursed words" that constantly ran in the background of her mind like empty Muzak, but a proper voice with its own logic and reason.

But he only had me cut down the soul of some strange monster overseas. He didn't let me love any humans.

♂♀

Just as Mikado Ryuugamine held a small secret—that he was the
founder of the Dollars—

Just as Masaomi Kida struggled with a big problem—as leader of the
Yellow Scarves—

Anri Sonohara had her own secret past hidden within her.

Saika.

A being without form in most cases.

It lurked within Anri Sonohara's right arm, singing accursed words
into her mind.

If she bothered to tell a doctor about this, any professional would
likely agree that the reason had to be within Anri herself—but as a
matter of fact, the source of the voice was completely outside of her
brain and did not stem from her own mind.

It was a being removed from rationality, neither physical nor mental
in nature.

Saika was what many considered to be a "cursed blade." It lurked
within Anri's body and could physically manifest as a katana at her
beck and call.

Anri, in fact, was the central figure behind a series of random slashings several months ago that the papers decided to label the "Night
of the Ripper." But she was not, in fact, responsible for the attacks
themselves—they were caused by offshoots that Saika had created.

Saika wanted "children" that served as proof of its love with human
beings. These children were created through a true curse, implanted
into the victims of the blade with a part of Saika's mind.

There was another girl that had been slashed before Anri became
Saika's host. The "child" of Saika implanted into that girl desired a
twisted love from humanity in the same way its parent did—and the
result of that rampage was the Night of the Ripper.

The incident was ultimately resolved when Anri brought all of those
"children" under her control. With the slashings stopped, she returned
the normal minds of all of those victims of Saika to their hosts, only

ensuring that their memories of the slashings reflected a more convenient story: No one who was slashed could remember the face of the attacker.

However, this incident sparked a conflict between the Yellow Scarves and the Dollars, plunging Anri's closest friends into a war without her realizing it.

♂♀

After all of this, Anri had accepted Saika but was not particularly happy about it.

Part of it was that it had caused the death of her parents, but mostly it was the unease of knowing that there were people out there aware of her state.

Saika's voice had returned to its normal chorus of *"I love you."* The reasoned, logical words she'd heard a second ago had been an occasional presence ever since the Night of the Ripper. And Anri suspected that Saika was speaking the truth.

She took a quiet breath and cautiously stared down the man in the gas mask.

"What do you know...and how much do you know...?"

"Ahh, well, if I were to answer that question, I would have to say that I know about you, *up to an extent*. But very well. As the saying goes, 'Even the starving hawk is too noble to ransack the crops,' and powerful beings like you would not prey upon weak little me, even if you were in trouble."

"...? Um, I'm afraid I don't..."

"At any rate, we can talk more upon that matter on another occasion. I am currently having a business conversation. Allow me to give you my card; you may contact me here."

The man in the gas mask pulled a business card out of his pocket and handed it to Anri.

"Nebula Pharmaceutical, Special Advisor: Shingen Kishitani," the card read, along with a number of methods of contact.

Anri looked at the card—her mind working fast—when she felt the pat of a hand on her shoulder from behind.

*   *   *

Instantly, a nasty sense of pressure engulfed her entire body.

A cold sharpness ran through her shoulder, and for a moment, time froze within her.

It felt like her freedom of movement had been stolen, like her body was being manhandled all over.

Gushk, gushk. Her nerves were gouged out.

Zig-zig-zig-zig. Her mind eerily creaked and cracked.

Zigshk, zigshk, zig-zig zig-zig zig zig-zig-zig zig-zig-zig-zig zig-zig-zig-zig zig-zig-zig-zig-zig-zig zig-zig zig-zig-zig   zig-zig-zig zig-zig-zig zig-zig-zig zig-zig zig-zig zig zig-zig zig-zig-zig-zig zig   zig zig-zig-zig-zig-zig-zig-zig-zig-zig-zig-zig-zig-zig-zig-zig-zig-zig-zig-zig-zig-zig-zig-zig-zig-zig-zig-zig-zig-zig-zig-zig-zig-zig-zig-zig-zig-zig—

The march of the ugly creaking reached its peak, and every cell in her body screamed, warning her of the danger of the man behind her.

Warning her that he was far, far more dangerous than she could imagine.

Anri slowly turned around, feeling cold sweat bloom from every pore of her body.

It was the smile of the white man, who had been watching the conversation from close by.

"Please forgive me, sweet little girl."

It was a smile meant to reassure and set at ease, but Anri's nerves stayed utterly taut. She stared him dead in the face.

"We are having a very important business conversation. Let me make it up to you by treating you to dinner sometime," he joked, pretending to hit on her. The man shook his head and moved in between Anri and Shingen.

"Oh...I see. I'm very sorry to interrupt," Anri said, burning the white man's face into her mind. She left the scene.

She mustn't forget that face. Her reason and instincts both told her so.

At the fork in the road leading to the underground tunnel, Anri turned back one last time.

The white man was still watching her.

She felt that twitching at her back and committed his face to memory one last time, just to be sure.

*   *   *

But ultimately, it was the last time she ever saw that face.

Because several hours later, Shizuo would hit him in the face with a bench, which meant that if he ever faced off with Anri again, he would look like a totally different person.

♂♀

Night, apartment, Ikebukuro

"The serial killer Hollywood...and they still haven't caught him? That's scary," said a boy to the TV inside his cheap apartment close to the train station.

Without anything better to do, Mikado decided that he would flip through the news on TV all day. The recent topic of interest to the media was the mysterious serial killer.

While the news itself did not report on the nickname, anyone who browsed the Internet or tabloid magazines was fully aware of the "Hollywood" moniker.

The first time he saw it covered on the news, it seemed like the events of some distant country, even though the incidents were taking place right there in the city. But through the Internet-enabled Hollywood nickname, the idle chats with friends, and the sites that popped up attempting to track down Hollywood's identity, he couldn't help but feel not just the fear of that eerie killer, but the tasteless, guilty allure of curiosity. Just who *was* Hollywood?

Society seemed more interested in the identity of the Black Rider than this mystery killer, but given that Mikado actually *knew* who the Headless Rider was, the still-unmasked Hollywood held much more fascination for him.

On the other hand, it seemed like following up a meeting with Anri by watching depressing news pieces only left a bad aftertaste. So he picked up the remote and muttered, "Maybe I can find a happier news segment."

As he surfed through the channels, he came across a report that

Yuuhei Hanejima's photo book had sold twenty thousand copies in its first week. On the screen was a portrait of a young man with far better looks than Mikado's.

"That's incredible. Twenty thousand copies at three thousand yen apiece... Even if he only makes ten percent in royalties, that's six million yen. And his movies are doing gangbusters. He's really got it all going on..."

He was inferior in every single way to the perfect superhuman on the screen. Mikado sighed dejectedly.

You know...I feel like this Yuuhei guy reminds me of someone I know...

The thought had occurred to him every time he saw the star actor, but no answer was forthcoming. Mikado continued flipping through every channel that was currently playing the news. Around the point that they all started covering the weather forecast, he decided it was time to check the TV guide in the paper.

With the schedule transition that April usually brought, most stations would be airing their own special programs starting in the next time block.

One of them was titled *Ikebukuro's 100-Day Front, Undercover! Shining a Light on the Hellhole That Is Ikebukuro, Live!*

Hellhole...? That seems unnecessarily harsh.

But he would be lying if he said he wasn't interested. In the end, Mikado decided to watch the show on the chance that he might see an acquaintance of his on live television.

Ultimately, his guess was correct.

But it was not the kind of acquaintance that he was expecting.

One hour later, he was watching a pitch-black shadow on the screen as it raced away from a motor officer.

"Celty...," he mumbled. He would never mistake that shadow for anyone else. He left the TV on and turned to the window.

The place they were showing on the program was not anywhere close, so naturally he couldn't see the events from his apartment. He tried to focus his ears to hear something, but that didn't turn up anything, either.

Meanwhile, Celty grew giant black wings on the screen and flew through the sky, like some kind of phantom thief.

"I don't know... That looks bad. Should I mobilize the Dollars...? I guess there's no way to do that," Mikado murmured, the very personification of the word *naive*. Back on the TV, they had returned to the news studio. He was worried for the sake of the inhuman dullahan that would normally have no connection to him whatsoever, but she was a member of the Dollars, after all.

"Well, I guess Celty can handle things for herself. Right?" he said and headed for the familiar chat room.

All the while, he was secretly harboring both excitement and anxiety over the Ikebukuro guided tour he would be leading the following evening.

Chat room

TarouTanaka has entered the chat.

TarouTanaka: Oh, no one's here.
TarouTanaka: I suppose I'll check back in a few hours.

TarouTanaka has left the chat.

The chat room is currently empty.

Bacura has entered the chat.

Bacura: Hmm?
Bacura: So nobody's here?
Bacura: Okay,
Bacura: Now I can write anything I damn well please on this unclaimed ground.
Bacura: Listen up, Johnny.
Bacura: When I was in elementary school,
Bacura: A girl in my class played my recorder.
Bacura: When I caught her in the act,
Bacura: In exchange for keeping her secret, I said,
Bacura: "What you really want to put your mouth on is my face."
Bacura: So rather than my recorder, she locked lips with my whistle instead.
Bacura: And when another boy saw it happen, he stuck his fingers in his mouth and tweeted away.
Bacura: HA-HA-HA
Bacura: It's both a true anecdote and an American-style joke!
Bacura: Cool,
Bacura: Now I just spam the chat to wash that backlog away.
Bacura: Sound off!

Saika has entered the chat.

Bacura: 1
Saika: good evening

Bacura: 2
Bacura: Eek!
Bacura: Evening.

TarouTanaka has entered the chat.

TarouTanaka: Good evening.
TarouTanaka: What are you doing, Bacura?
Bacura: Good...eve...
Bacura: C'mon, laugh.
Bacura: Everybody laugh at meeee!
TarouTanaka: Aha-ha-ha-ha-ha-ha-ha-ha-ha-ha-ha-ha.
Bacura: You're really laughing?!

Kuru has entered the chat.
Mai has entered the chat.

Kuru: I do not approve of the act of mocking a person upon your first meeting, but as you have requested it yourself, and I believe that the proper act as a human being in this case is to laugh at you long and loud, I am prepared to mock you as mercilessly and thoroughly as I can manage. And now...
Mai: (lol)
Kuru: Kya-ha-ha-ha-ha-ha-ha-ha-ha-ha-ha-ha-ha-ha-ha-ha! Ah-haaa. ♪ Aha, ah-ha-ha! Fweh...fweh-heh... Kya-haaa! Kya-ha-ha-ha-ha-ha-ha-ha-ha-ha! Aaaa-ha-ha-ha-ha-ha-ha-ha-ha-ha-ha-ha! Ah-ha-ha, ah-ha-ha! Wai...sto...stop! It's too funny! It's really funny...stop...no, please, let me goooo! Hee...hee...aha...kya-hee... Kya-ha-ha-ha-ha-ha-ha-ha-ha!
Mai: (lol)
Bacura: Evening...
Bacura: Wait,
Bacura: Who are you?!
Bacura: Wow, you sure found a way to laugh that causes both despair and rage!
TarouTanaka: Good evening.
TarouTanaka: Is this our first meeting?
Saika: good evening

Kuru: Please forgive me. This is the first time that I have met everyone here. We will be visiting this chat room occasionally from this point onward and have come to pay our respects. My name is Kuru. Normally, I would have introduced myself as the first point of order, but I believed that it would have been rude to Bacura to put my introduction before the mockery of his very impassioned joke.

Mai: I'm Mai.

Bacura: You seem a lot like Kanra to me.

Mai: I'm sorry.

Bacura: I wasn't talking about you.

TarouTanaka: It's nice to meet the two of you.

Kuru: The pleasure is all mine. By the way, Bacura, it occurred to me that you might be a woman...and if that were the case, the recorder would have been shared by two girls, leading to a kiss between females, the aesthetically pleasing and tantalizing image of which is now saved in my mind. It has put me into a state of, shall we say, trancelike ecstasy.

Mai: Naughty.

Bacura: I'll leave it up to your imagination.

TarouTanaka: Great, more weirdos...

Saika: its nice to meet you

Bacura: Oh yeah, did you see that thing on TV a few hours ago?

TarouTanaka: The one about Ikebukuro?

Bacura: Yeah, that one.

Saika: did something happen

TarouTanaka: The Headless Rider was caught on camera during a live broadcast.

Kuru: Oh, what a coincidence. We were just viewing that program as well and went outside to perhaps catch sight of the Headless Rider before coming back in and joining this chat room. Unfortunately we were not able to witness the living urban legend in the flesh, but the pleasure of walking the streets at night with that hope in mind was an indescribable thrill.

Mai: Too bad.

TarouTanaka: Oh, so you two are from Ikebukuro as well?

TarouTanaka: Pretty much everyone who uses this chat is from Ikebukuro or Shinjuku.

TarouTanaka: Well, enjoy yourselves.

Kuru: I am most humbly grateful, Mr. TarouTanaka, for the truly kind hospitality that you have shown to such an inconsiderate boor who is nothing more than mineral deposits on a grain of sand in the ocean that is the Internet. I believe I might even fall in love. But only on the Internet.

Mai: Thanks.

Mai: Love you.

TarouTanaka: I don't know how to respond to this, ha-ha.

Bacura: I have a feeling Kanra is punking us...

Saika: what is punking

Bacura: It means this is all a hidden-camera prank.

TarouTanaka: At any rate, tomorrow I'll be around Ikebukuro, guiding and being guided.

TarouTanaka: I'm still a newcomer to this city, so it's good to meet you.

Kuru: That is a coincidence. We, too, have plans to travel through Ikebukuro tomorrow. Perhaps we might even meet face-to-face and fist-to-fist.

Mai: We're gonna punch 'em?

TarouTanaka: If we do, go easy on me, lol.

The next morning, in front of Animate, Ikebukuro

There is a short passage from the intersection to the west of the Sunshine building until you reach National Route 254. This stretch includes a number of shops that sell fan-made *doujinshi* and merchandise explicitly aimed at females, which earned it the name Otome (Maiden) Road.

On this sunny afternoon, two boys and a girl strolled down that very street. The girl was Karisawa, and one of the boys was Yumasaki.

The other male, who served as both guardian and brake system for the other two, was Kyouhei Kadota. He kept his knit cap pulled low and listened to the conversation of the pair walking behind him. Though to be honest, he was only concentrating on about half of it.

"That's the thing. What I think is, you *should* argue about your opinions of an anime. If each side debates its side logically, it can only help the other. But the people who prop up their favorite anime by saying, 'If you don't get what makes this good, just watch your panty-shot anime instead' are the worst, and they don't realize that they're indirectly insulting the very anime they claim to like so much."

"Oh yeah. There were people saying that on the official forum for the *Gunjaws!* anime. I understand that you get mad when people make fun of you, but why bring another genre down to get back?"

"Exactly! I love hard-core series that have nothing but dudes in them, and I also love moe series full of panty shots and nip slips—*hbwah?!*"

"Yumacchi, you dummy!"

Karisawa abruptly slapped him on the cheek. He looked at her, stunned. "Wh-what was that for, Karisawa?"

"Claiming that moe anime means panty shots and nip slips is only going to cause misunderstandings! Moe is defined by the soul of the viewer! In that sense, it applies to every piece of animation in the entire world! Even the ancient animal illustrations of the *Choju-giga* are excellent moe scrolls, and you're here limiting it to—"

"No, you don't understand! When I'm speaking of panty shots being connected to moe, I'm only speaking of a particular method, while also encompassing all of the romance and fantasy of——"

"——at my stage, I can find every male character in *Gunjaws!* to be moe——"

"————————Karisawa, I think you've got the wrong idea about——
————"

"————moe————moe————moe————moe-moe——"
"————moe————moe-moe?————moe————————"

As they droned on and on, their companion finally broke his silence.

"Please, you two, just stop talking about your moe stuff out in public like this," Kadota pleaded, sighing and pressing his forehead with his fingers.

Whether in the warmth of April or the chill of winter, the topic of conversation for those two never changed. If anything did change, it was merely the title of whatever anime or manga they were discussing.

"Can't you just get off the topic of 2-D stuff already?"

"Sure thing."

"Tsk."

Surprised that they actually obliged him, Kadota was delighted to have some silence. It lasted only a second.

"By the way, the figures that the sculptor Zetsumu Youen makes have been getting sexier around the waistline lately, don't you think?"

"No, it's the barely raised stomach lines that show off the ribs of his slender characters that are the true moe his style inspires!"

It was the exact same stuff as before. Kadota bellowed, "I *just* told you to stop talking about that!"

Yumasaki and Karisawa were taken aback by his anger.

"What do you mean?! Figures are 3-D!"

"Not quite, Karisawa! Figures are actually 2.5-D!"

"…When I'm with you, sometimes I wonder if this is actually Japan at all," Kadota grumbled, half-resigned. He resumed walking toward his destination: the Tokyu Hands department store.

When they rounded a corner and the pedestrian traffic wasn't so thick, he turned back and asked, "It's tonight, right? You're gonna take Mikado and whoever around those stores and stuff?"

"Yeah, that's right. Wanna come?"

"Nah, I'd only scare them away."

"You think so, Dotachin? If you took your cap off and laid your bangs flat, you'd make a pretty convincing honor student!" Karisawa teased. Kadota ignored her and kept walking—until he saw something unfamiliar.

*   *   *

"See, we're just askin' questions, yeah? Askin' if you know anything about the Black Rider, yeah?"

"You girls want money, right? Well, so do we. So don't hog all of it, yeah?"

"Why don't you invest some allowance in us? If we score the ten million yen, we'll pay you back physically. With interest."

"Yeah, and we're almost the same age as you, so it won't count as prostitution. Seriously. I'll even do it for free."

A group of men chanting extremely stereotypical taunts had surrounded two teenage girls. Each of the men wore imposing, tough-looking clothes, and one of them was in a full motorcycle-gang uniform with stripes.

"Awright, I get it. You girls are the Black Rider."

"Yeah, that's it."

"That'd be hilarious."

"So why don't you have ten-million-yen worth of fun with us?"

The content of their taunts and challenges were like a slice from another period in time. It made them seem quite out of place in the big city.

Kadota watched the men for a bit, then muttered, "I never expected to see such stereotypical street thugs in this day and age." The trio strode forward, shaking their heads.

Meanwhile, the men hadn't noticed their observers. They continued to harass the girls.

"Actually, if you two hang out in this neighborhood, you must be pretty loaded, huh?"

"Filthy. Filthy!"

"C'mon, don't just clam up. Say something, huh?"

"Hang on, you guys. Don't you see they're scared? Sorry about that. As an apology, why don't we take you somewhere you want to go? Huh?"

When one of the thugs started to initiate a weak attempt at a good-cop-bad-cop routine, Kadota decided it was time to open his mouth.

♂♀

Several hours later, in front of Tokyu Hands

The few days surrounding Raira Academy's extended break were half days that ended at noon. It was meant to smooth out the transition between vacation and study, but the students just thought, *I get to hang out all afternoon, yay*, which was, in a way, the point.

When the day's curriculum ended, the town overflowed with Raira uniforms. The school allowed for personal clothes to be worn, so once out in the town, those students melted into the crowd, while the uniform wearers stood out as a distinct group. Almost like a color gang.

Mikado slowly strode through the neighborhood, wearing that very uniform. When he reached his destination, Anri and his junior at school were already there.

"Oh? You made it before me? Sorry, were you waiting long?"

"No, I just got here."

"Me, too."

Anri and Aoba both seemed a bit reserved, and they didn't appear to have been talking before he arrived. It was probably true that they had just gotten there before him. Once the greetings were out of the way, Aoba bowed to the both of them.

"I'm sorry about this. I'm just using up your valuable free time with my own selfish request…"

"That's not true. We didn't have anything to do, either," Mikado said. Anri nodded.

The younger boy looked thankful at their thoughtfulness, then piped up curiously, "Mr. Ryuugamine and Ms. Sonohara, are you a couple?"

Time stopped between the two.

To someone who was just meeting them, this seemed like a perfectly normal assumption. Aoba had specifically asked Mikado for a tour of Ikebukuro, and yet here was Anri as well. It was only natural to assume that there was a romantic bond there or at least something more than just classmates.

Mikado was clearly stunned by the question, while Anri looked down, her cheeks pink. It was hard to tell if they were confirming or denying that accusation, so Aoba watched them curiously and asked, "Am I wrong?"

"N-no-no-no, it's not like that… We're still just, um, friends. Friends!"

"Ohh. Does that mean you're available now, Ms. Sonohara? Shall I nominate myself for the position?"

"Wha—!"

Mikado found himself actually feeling admiration for the boy's straight-faced lack of caution.

How can he just...say that? And he comes off even smoother than Masaomi!

Mikado's lips trembled, ready to say something...but no words emerged. He was racked with both frustration that a younger schoolmate beat him to the punch and respect for the boy's game in putting himself out there to the opposite sex.

The younger boy turned to his immobile senior and hesitantly clarified, "Um, Mr. Ryuugamine, you know that was a joke, right?"

"Huh?"

"I mean, you don't have to look like the world is crumbling around your ears..."

"...Did...did I look like that?" Mikado asked, going red with embarrassment. He glanced sidelong at Anri. In her usual way, she was looking awkwardly at the ground, listening to the conversation.

The pair looked like bashful little kids. Meanwhile, the one who looked closest to an actual kid laughed and whispered to Mikado, "I'm glad. I thought since you were with the Dollars, you would have a scary side...but I'm happy to know that someone like you is in the group."

"I dunno. I mean, I appreciate that, but..."

Huh? That was a compliment, right? Mikado wondered, unsure if it was meant to be sarcastic. He smiled politely.

Emboldened by the effect of his last question, Aoba decided to push further. "So...are the people we're going to meet today also Dollars?"

"Well, yes...but don't worry, they're not scary, either."

Not scary in the way you're thinking, at least, Mikado thought, imagining the machine-gun chatter that was Yumasaki and Karisawa's specialty. He looked around, checking to see if they were approaching.

But their next visitors were not the nerdy duo.

"Do you have a moment?"

"We'd like to pray for your happiness."

On either side of Mikado was a tall man approaching six feet.

"—?! H-h-how can I help you?"

"Just let me see your face."

The tall men grabbed him without permission, their manner suddenly cruel.

"This the guy?"

"Yep, that's him! Bingo. Got confirmation."

The men looked at each other happily, whatever their "bingo" was. Based on the lip piercings and crooked teeth black from nicotine, they did not appear to be pacifists. Mikado was a believer in not judging a book by its cover, but in this one situation, he felt confident that these books were exactly what their covers suggested.

As Aoba and Anri watched in stunned confusion, the men leered gleefully and leaned in toward Mikado, their faces reeking of cigarette smoke.

"Hey. You were there, right? You were there recently?"

"Th-there…? Where?"

"You were there, ya know? You were at that junked factory with the Black Rider that one time that Kadota's group kicked the shit outta us. Yeah?"

"Did you get a little sloppy today, just 'cuz we weren't wearin' yellow?"

"…!"

The mention of the word *yellow* plunged Mikado's mind into chaos.

"…You must be…"

The remnants of the Yellow Scarves?!

But these were not the proper Yellow Scarves that Masaomi had gathered to his side. They were the leftovers of a gang called the Blue Squares who had infiltrated the Yellow Scarves in a takeover attempt. They were ultimately crushed by a different infiltration team led by Kadota.

"Well, whatever. We don't care why you were there when it happened."

"It's just, we want the ten million yen, ya know?"

Ten million yen.

That was the last piece of the puzzle to click into place. They weren't coming after Mikado to enact revenge against a member of the Dollars…

"You know where that Black Rider is, don'cha? Huh?!"

"Let's go. You can donate your cell to our cause, huh? Got the phone number right in there, I bet."

They crudely grabbed at his bag, yanking it open to pore over the contents.

"Wait…stop that!"

"Shuddup!"

Mikado tried to resist, but he was hopelessly outsized and didn't have the combat training to make up for it. Just when he was afraid that the six-foot-tall giants would steal his cell phone—

"Hiii, Mikah-do."

A shadow loomed behind the men, a head taller than even they were.

"?!"

"Wh-what the...fu...uh...?"

It was an enormous black man in a white T-shirt. For an instant, Mikado wasn't sure who it was, either, but he recognized the man within moments. The lack of the sushi-chef outfit was what threw him off, but in fact, the man was quite a recognizable figure in the area.

"Simon!"

"What wrong? Fight is no good. You get hungrily-hungrily. Our sushi shop closed today. So you fight, you starve."

"H-hey! Leggo..."

"C-can't move..."

He was only holding the shoulders of the two men, but they struggled as if they were trapped at the bottom of the ocean. They couldn't even budge their own fingers.

Despite the incredible pressure he was exerting on them, Simon's expression was as cool as a cucumber. "You pick up bag. Leave these ruffians to me and run to safe-tee," he said in the style of some kind of samurai movie, his pronunciation as awkward and endearing as ever.

It was the kind of line that usually signaled an imminent death, but in this case, that fate was more likely for his hapless victims.

"B-but Simon..."

"You no fight when girl around. Run to *Thirty-Six Views of Mount Fuji*, go, go, go."

"Th-thank you! We'll all come have sushi soon!"

"Ohh, very good. In thanks, I charge you only ten percent interest on market price."

It probably came out more intimidating than what Simon meant to say. Meanwhile, Mikado picked up his bag, grabbed Aoba and Anri, and raced off.

As they ran through the streets of Ikebukuro, Mikado bowed to Anri and his schoolmate.

"S-sorry! I didn't mean for you to get dragged into that nonsense!"

"Um, dragged into? You were the only one who suffered any consequences," Aoba noted. Mikado found that he was right, but he couldn't help but feel ashamed and embarrassed that they'd been put through that frightening experience anyway.

It was his first underclassman since coming to high school. Did he just get carried away because of all the reverential gazes Aoba was giving him? Did he get cocky and think he was cooler than he really was?

There was plenty of time to regret, but no time to reflect.

From out of the alleys came a group of men who must have been alerted by the previous punks via cell phone.

"Hey, what about the other guys?!"

"Forget 'em! We couldn't beat Simon with our entire group, and starting a brawl there will only draw Shizuo's attention!" the men yelled as they chased after the trio.

The distance was short enough that they could catch up in twenty seconds if they sprinted. But unluckily for them and luckily for Mikado, this was the area where the students were supposed to be meeting their friends.

"Eep!" Mikado shrieked when the van suddenly stopped in front of them, thinking that it was a fresh round of pursuers. But then he recognized the man in the passenger seat, and his face lit up.

"K-Kadota!"

The next moment, Karisawa poked her head out of the door and yelled, "Why are you being chased?! Anyway, get in, get in!"

Just in the nick of time, Mikado, Anri, and Aoba piled into the van and shut the door before the thugs could reach them.

Togusa started the engine at the exact same moment. One of the thugs reached for the handle of the passenger-side door, but Kadota's fist flew out of the open window and put a stop to that.

"Y-you—you—you saved us!"

"Hey, it's all good. Sorry for being late to our meeting spot!" Karisawa said, cackling.

The van was surprisingly cramped, with the rear being taken up by Mikado's trio, Karisawa, and Yumasaki—and a pair of girls who Mikado did not recognize.

The girls in the very back of the van were possibly twins, because aside from one having glasses, they looked exactly the same.

"Um...what are you two doing in here?" Aoba Kuronuma asked, surprised.

They know each other? Mikado wondered, but before he could say anything, they heard an obnoxious horn from outside and a dull thud against the side of the van.

"Damn, they found us," the driver grunted, irritated. Mikado looked out of the side windows. He thought the Yellow Scarves they'd ditched had caught up in their own car, but instead, what he saw through the tinted windows was a gang of modified motorcycles bearing men in striped gang uniforms.

"Stop the damn caaaah!"

"Gonna fry ya up in motor oiiil!"

"What happened to our backup?!"

"They can't come; they found the Black Rider! We're supposed to join *them* now!"

The gang of bikers shouted back and forth among themselves, but Mikado couldn't make out their messages from within the van.

"Wh-what's going on? What's happening right now?"

"Well, you see, I have an unfortunate announcement. You basically jumped out of the frying pan and into the fire. Too bad, so sad. We are currently inhabiting a troubled dimension just as treacherous as a certain academy city researching supernatural powers. We'll just have to wait for the saga of the one whose right hand will bring down this ugly illusion..."

"What in the world are you talking about?!"

"Let me just make sure: Do you know any doctors who look like a frog? That'll bump your odds of survival up about ten percent. Actually, speaking of frogs, Hakusan Meikun would work, as well."

Mikado gave up on interacting with Yumasaki's utter nonsense and turned to Kadota in the front passenger seat instead. When their eyes met through the rearview mirror, the older man looked a bit apologetic.

"Yeah, some...stuff happened. Sorry."

"Wh-whaaaaat?!"

Thus began a guided tour of Ikebukuro that was more thrilling than anyone asked for.

The group was locked into a deadly chase without a finish line.

Just at the moment that the next step was impossible to predict (if you even wanted to)—

They heard the whinnying of a headless horse approaching from the front.

CHAPTER 3
WAKAHIME CLUB
"THE HOTTEST SPRING IN THE WORLD! THE EROTIC TERMINAL OF HIGH SCHOOL GIRLS, IKEBUKURO!"

"A dripping blackboard eraser! The after-school extracurricular activities never stop when the town becomes your campus! Tokyo's dangerous horizon wafting with the scent of shining roses, Ikebukuro...

A proud eagle wanders the heights, seeking to slake her ashen lust—the high school girl!

Among these girls who caress the borderline between passion and destruction, our special reporter witnessed a rare sight: the 'yamanba' crone fairy!"

Thus read the shameless front cover of *Wakahime (Young Princess) Club*, an adult magazine. It was meant to focus on a certain subset of youth culture and package it for consumption to an older audience, but this particular publication, owing to its very peculiar angle and marketing, was well known for trailblazing its own very niche direction.

On the cover were two women in school sailor uniforms, clearly well over twenty years old, posed in a provocative manner, with a number of holy Buddhist seals placed on their legs below their skirts.

On the center foldout, the seals came into play once again, covering the most sensitive feminine area in a photo that was as erotic as it was confusing.

It was difficult enough to look at a pornographic magazine in front of others—particularly in a classroom when there were girls around—but the obviously slanted aesthetic of this one made it especially awkward.

But in a first-year classroom at Raira Academy, one person read this magazine right out in the open.

"Oooh. Ahhh. Ohhh. That's hot. Very nice. Wish I had this body, ya know?"

This figure, leaning back in her chair and smirking to herself, was clad in a black-based school uniform that did not belong to Raira Academy. She wore glasses and had a simple smile without a hint of cosmetics covering it. In short, she looked just like a bookworm who should be hiding in a corner of the library, poring over the literary greats like Natsume Soseki or Osamu Dazai.

"Oh man, that's good stuff. How do you get boobs this big? Milk? Is it milk? What if you just pour the milk right on the boobs and then rub it into the skin? Will that help? What do you think?" she asked the boy sitting next to her with a dazzling smile.

The boy being questioned turned red with a look that said, *Why are you asking me?* and flopped down onto his desk, glancing at her.

While they both had glasses, this girl was the polar opposite of Anri Sonohara otherwise. While Anri had a calm, shadowy maturity to her, this girl had eyes that flashed with mischief behind the lenses and the natural brightness of personality to match it.

And this girl was the one gleefully flipping through the porno mag.

She had a long black skirt and thick glasses, a combination that screamed "honor student." Not the type of girl you would expect to read something like *that*.

But she continued rifling through the centerfold pictures with an innocent smile on her face, dropping unwanted comments to the boys on either side of her desk.

The boys didn't know what to do. They were utterly at the mercy of a girl they'd only met half an hour earlier.

♂♀

Raira Academy, first day of school

Raira Academy was a coed private high school in southern Ikebukuro.

It had a different name just a few years earlier, but it earned its current name when it merged with another local high school.

The campus grounds were not that large, but the school maximized the use of what space it had, so it didn't feel cramped. It was also close to Ikebukuro Station, which made it an attractive school to people from the suburbs of Tokyo who wanted to commute from home. The average test score and difficulty of getting in were on a slow rise, and its past rumors of being quite a slum before the merger were now a distant memory.

There was a nice view of the surrounding terrain from the higher-altitude campus, but the looming sixty-floor building just ahead did not brook any feeling of superiority. On the other side of the school was Zoshigaya Cemetery, which gave it a slightly lonely atmosphere for being in the middle of a metropolitan city.

Of course, when the students were there, that lonely feeling was nowhere to be seen, crowded out by the oasis of youth at the heart of the capital.

After the school opening ceremonies were finished, each classroom got down to the business of student introductions.

But among them were a few notable outliers.

First, every class had to have its clown—someone who looked for laughs in the hope of livening up the room or sometimes fell on their face and just made things awkward. Some of them were so dense that they couldn't even realize their jokes weren't landing.

While some stood out intentionally in their search for stardom, others couldn't help but stick out by virtue of their size or looks. Others flubbed their own names when doing introductions, which quickly slapped them with the "ditzy" tag.

The Ritual of the First Impression presented a largely insurmountable wall to others, to varied emotional reactions.

Given the nature of the academy, it was rare for people to wind up being classmates with kids they'd been with since middle school or even earlier. Excluding classmates from Raira Academy Middle

School or the other junior highs in the immediate area, you were lucky if you had one or two old friends in your class.

So the mask of the first impression was surprisingly heavy in regard to its effect on one's personal relationships for the next year (or three). People are more than their appearances suggest, as the saying goes, but that quote held no water if there wasn't someone around capable of seeing that inner personality, and there was no guarantee that such understanding confidants would be among one's classmates.

The first impression would lead to the creation of social groups and exert a powerful influence over lunch cliques, classwork teams, and other gatherings.

It all came down to whether you could blend into the class or not. That was the ritual being held when a student made his or her introduction to the rest of the class: the first test of the school year.

And whether they realized this importance or not, there were two students who clearly did not pick up on the signals.

♂♀

One was the bespectacled girl in Class 1-B.

"I'm Mairu Orihara! Orihara is spelled with the characters for *fold* and *field*, while Mairu means 'dance' and 'flow.' Nice to meet you! My favorite books are the encyclopedia, manga, and porn mags!"

Her introduction itself was brief and ordinary enough that most of her classmates took the final bit as a forced joke. But her black uniform stood out quite a bit among the green-based Raira uniforms.

What she said next, however, completely changed the feeling in the room.

"I go for both teams when it comes to love and lust! But the spot in my bed for men is already spoken for, so don't even try! I can go out with as many girls as I want, however, so keep that in mind when you propose a relationship!"

♂♀

The other student was a girl in Class 1-C who also stood out quite a bit.

"Kururi...Orihara."

Despite it being the first day of school, she was wearing gym clothes, which immediately made her stick out like a sore thumb. Raira allowed its students to wear their own clothes even at official ceremonies, but most kids chose to play it safe and wear the official uniform or jacket.

Yet this girl wanted to wear gym clothes.

As she started to sit back down, the teacher asked, "Is there anything else you wish to say about yourself?"

"No, there isn't...," she said in a tiny voice, then sluggishly sat down.

The thin fabric of her shirt accentuated the size of her breasts, which, combined with her taut limbs, attracted the gaze of all the male students.

But given that her personality was already questionable based on her choice of outfits to the ceremony, none of the boys opted to stare for too long, lest they attract the disgust of the other girls in the class.

She had a healthy, vibrant outfit and figure. But her expression and manner were gloomy and sickly.

After telling the class nothing but her name, the girl quietly sat down in her seat and resumed staring at her desk.

A boy sitting to one side of her—Aoba Kuronuma—glanced at the girl in the strange outfit and idly thought, *She seems gloomy. But what's with the gym clothes?*

That was the extent of his curiosity, however. He looked around and noticed other boys sending curious glances at the girl and looks of disgust from the girls in the class.

Well, as long as she doesn't get picked on.

But that would ultimately be her problem, not his. Attention turned to the next student's introduction—not just from Aoba, but from most of the class.

There was just one student adrift from the crowd, that was all. Eventually, the remaining classmates turned their attention to the continuing introductions, and that was all they thought of it.

♂♀

Given that they were in separate classes, the rest of the school didn't realize that the two odd girls who appeared in Class B and Class C, if you ignored their glasses, hairstyle, and bust size, had essentially the same face and build.

There was also the matter of the last name Orihara.

The teachers who had been around since before the name change to Raira experienced an instinctual *danger* signal when they saw that name.

"Well...just because he was their brother doesn't mean they're just like him. It wouldn't be right to discriminate against them because of that," a veteran art teacher said, sipping tea in the faculty room. "But...compared to when Izaya and Shizuo were here, it's so much more peaceful now."

The elderly teacher grinned wryly, thinking back on the problem child of the past wistfully.

"We don't have barrels of gasoline rolling down the third-floor hallway anymore, for one thing."

♂♀

At that moment, apartment building, Shinjuku

"Now that I think about it," Namie said with a softer than usual expression, but without stopping her work, "today is the entrance ceremony and start of school for Raira Academy."

She sounded oddly happy about it. Izaya did not look up from organizing his e-mail, however. "That's right. But why would you bring that up out of the blue?"

"Seiji's starting his second year of high school... I wish I could have rushed to the ceremony to celebrate with him..."

"The first day of school? He's in his second year, so parents and guardians have nothing to do with it."

"Well, I want to see it," Namie answered without hesitation. Izaya shook his head in disbelief. Namie normally played the role of the cool-headed beauty, but when it came to her younger brother, Seiji Yagiri, she proudly exhibited a level and depth of love that was abnormal.

It wasn't the platonic love of a family, but the physical, lusty love between a man and woman. But her brother reciprocated none of that; in fact, he seemed to find her obnoxious. Yet even those cold glances were lovable to Namie.

A look of bliss stole over her suddenly pink cheeks as she imagined her brother growing up, and she continued her work in a better mood than before.

Izaya glanced at his assistant, sighed, and muttered, "Raira Academy... That place has totally changed since they merged and got a new name."

"Oh, you went there?"

"I graduated about six or seven years ago. Back then, it was just Raijin High School."

For an instant, Izaya smiled with wistful longing—and the expression turned to a cruel, hateful smirk just as quickly.

"But...it was all horrible there, including the fact that it's where I met Shizu."

"You really do hate him, don't you?" Namie replied, then had an idea. "If you graduated high school six or seven years ago... Didn't you say that you're twenty-one right now?"

"I've been telling people I'm twenty-one for several years. Do you really think I'd just give out personal information like that?"

She ignored him, exasperated, then abruptly stopped and turned to look at him. "Does that mean you do trust me a bit?"

"I wouldn't call it trust. It's more like giving out just a little bit of information to keep a subordinate from leading a mutiny."

"You ought to die," she spat, returning to her work. "By the way, your sisters are starting school there today, too," she shot back.

"...I'm surprised you know that." Izaya's face went just a bit hard.

"I can do a bit of research on the king I serve, too."

"...Fine. It's the same thing I do to you."

He didn't like the turnabout, a fact he made clear with a pained grimace. Eventually, he gave up on his work and leaned back in the chair to mutter, "I don't know how to handle those two."

"Oh? To think that you would have trouble handling anyone other than Shizuo Heiwajima."

"Don't tease me. I'm only human, you know? I'm not perfect," Izaya said, sighing heavily. He began to explain some of his background to her. "My sisters…who are named Kururi and Mairu, by the way… Well, my parents are normal. Except for their naming choices. But I was raised in normal circumstances—and turned out like this."

"So you're aware that you're a freak."

He ignored Namie's barb and folded his hands, entwining his fingers. "I turned out weird, despite my normal upbringing. But them, on the other hand—I feel like they turned out weird because of my influence. I won't deny that I feel a bit of responsibility for that."

"What do you mean by weird?"

What are those girls like, if this freak thinks they're weird? Namie wondered, stopping her work for a minute to pour some tea from the teapot in the kitchen. She stood there, ready to hear more, which prompted a tired look from Izaya.

"What they're trying to be is…human."

"…Huh?"

"They want to represent the human being in a microcosm. The Japanese human being, specifically."

"I don't understand what you mean," she said cautiously. Izaya's grimace was barely visible.

"It's a very difficult task they've set. Basically, they think that as twins, they make up one person."

"…I see. It often feels like twins add up to a single life-form when taken together, from our perspective. But…I suppose other twins would find that idea quite offensive."

"Normally, perhaps. But as I said, my sisters are not normal."

Izaya closed the laptop and steadily got to his feet. He flicked the window blinds open and narrowed his eyes at the light that filtered through.

"You know how video games have character parameters? Stats, and so on. They say that you're good at magic but terrible at fighting or a good brawler but a total nimrod. When you make up a party in an RPG, you have to balance that party out, so that each person makes up for the others' shortcomings."

"That's not so different from reality. The very first step to rational optimization is ensuring each person has the right role."

"If only it were an issue of rationality." Izaya leaned over and put his hands on the table, envisioning his sisters. "Anyway, they're trying to create this RPG party themselves. As if one were the fighter and the other were the magician."

"...I don't understand what you mean."

"It's simple. They decided to intentionally fashion different personalities for themselves. They actively turned themselves into identical twins with totally different personas! And they assume that by acting together, this makes them better... They're under the illusion that they can do *anything* that way."

He grinned as though seeing something funny, but there was no humor in his eyes. "When they were in elementary school, they chose their looks and personality at random. With no regard to logicality! That's why Kururi, the elder of the two, plays the silent, gloomy type, despite her gym clothes outfit. And Mairu the younger is a bright and talkative character, yet she looks like a bookworm."

"But...that makes no sense. Why would you separate your looks and personalities?" Namie wondered, stunned.

Izaya nodded. "Exactly. It makes no sense. But to them, having your appearance and personality match doesn't make sense to begin with. In the end, they're still combining themselves into one person. They think that as long as all the parts are present, there's no problem. They're just special enough that they can pull it off. I mean, talk about a bad case of eighth-grader syndrome."

"What's eighth-grader syndrome?"

"Just do a search on it. I mean, they could have it worse—they could claim that they can use psychic powers or they were warriors of light in a past life—but at any rate, they find a way to stand out, no matter the group."

"I see. And given your desire to be the hidden puppet master, you'd prefer to be far away from them," Namie calmly surmised.

He looked away, surprised at being pinned so accurately. "Anyway, it makes you embarrassed just to listen to them talk. I'm sure you'll understand if you ever meet them... It's *really* painful. And that's coming from me, so you know it's true."

"If you already understand that you belong within the realm of painfully embarrassing people, I'd hope you would act on that information."

"I'd prefer not to get that lecture from a woman who did plastic surgery on an unwilling girl for the sake of her own brother," Izaya shot back.

Her lips bared in a tiny smile. "I have absolutely no intention of coming clean to Seiji."

"..."

"Didn't you know that love doesn't need an accelerator or a brake? Just caring about the other person puts you right at their side," she answered—though it wasn't an answer at all—her cheeks glowing a rosy red. Namie looked like the very picture of a slightly older maiden in love.

If only it wasn't with her own little brother, Izaya thought, leaning back into his chair.

Namie turned to him, her expression proper again, and asked, "Will they be all right? Kids who stick out like these guys are likely to be bullied, don't you think? And the bullies these days are quite nasty."

The words themselves were full of sympathy and care for Izaya's relatives, but her voice was completely devoid of emotion. She clearly did not actually care.

Izaya, meanwhile, only seemed half-interested for his part. He conjectured, "I suppose. I hope there's no bullying...but I very much doubt that."

The information broker sighed...then grinned.

"The poor things."

♂♀

Three days later, noon, Raira Academy

Why does bullying happen?

Aoba Kuronuma pondered the issue from his seat in the back of the classroom. It was said that the reason bullying happened lay as much in the bullied as the bully, but in reality, that didn't really matter, did it?

The pressures of society, the influence of video games, too much manga, bad parents, bad schools, bad Internet.

None of this mattered, thought Aoba.

There were probably an infinite number of reasons, and removing every last one of them still wouldn't stop a bully from doing what he did. It all happened because they were making themselves feel better.

The people who couldn't help themselves from feeling better were the ones who went on to engage in bullying. It was a bit of a forced conclusion, but despite knowing how simplified it was, Aoba decided to follow that line of thinking.

I don't try to hide it. It feels good to bully those weaker than me. The only question is whether I can resist that pleasure or not.

It was like fighting a country with nothing but foot soldiers and bombarding them with missiles from a safe distance. All the idealistic speeches in the world couldn't change the fact that it felt good to be safe and know that you were superior to the other person.

And those who watch without stopping it are feeling both the fear of retribution and the relief that they weren't the ones singled out.

That's right. Just being in a place of safety is a kind of pleasure. Sure, there are probably total saints out there who don't feel any pleasure from that and just want to help others. Given how many people are on the planet, it would be weird if there weren't.

But...I don't think there are any in this class.

And so, just before the last homeroom session of the day started at the very end of school, Aoba glanced over at Kururi Orihara's desk, which sat adjacent to his.

A number of pieces of graffiti had been left on it in permanent marker.

Wow, only three days into the school year?

However, the content of the messages was not quite like the normal methods of bullying.

"Sister of the slut"

"Take responsibility!"

"Abandonment of guardian duty!"

"Prostitute sisters"

"Leave the ranks of the living!"

The messages were surprisingly verbose, with some choice vocabulary words. For her part, Kururi just stared down at the desk. The crime had happened during the twenty minutes that she was away at the library.

Kururi might stick out like a sore thumb with her gym clothes and gloomy personality—but almost none of the insults directly referenced her.

Why would so many of the messages be directed not at her, but her sister, Mairu Orihara?

The reason why happened earlier that morning.

♂♀

"Good morning!"

On the third day of school, Mairu Orihara walked into class to find that her desk was covered in graffiti saying things like "slut" and "one thousand yen for a ride" and "will put out for cash."

She paused, grunted, and looked around the classroom with a smile frozen on her face.

Every single person in the classroom had his or her back to her, pretending not to be aware of the state of her desk. They were acting as if they didn't see her at all.

It was a classic bullying tactic.

But she just continued to calmly watch the rest of the class...until she settled on one member of the girls' group near the window at the front of the class. One of the girls had glanced at her sidelong and then snorted and whispered something to the others.

Instantly, Mairu's mouth bent into a grin. But not the smile of gentle pleasure—it was the sharp and nasty leer of a con man with a fresh sucker in his sights on the otherwise attractive girl's face.

She leaped.

It all lasted only a second.

Something on the floor exploded. But that was only in the minds of the students; there was no explosion, only the sound of Mairu slamming her foot against the floor as she leaped.

In the minds of those bullying—or avoiding becoming involved in it by ignoring the whole affair—Mairu Orihara was supposed to be invisible and utterly absent from the room. It took all of 0.05 seconds for that illusion to be shattered.

By the time everyone swung around to see the source of the sound, Mairu was off the floor and in the air at the back of the room. She landed on a desk behind her with one foot, using it as a launching pad to propel herself on top of the locker against the back wall. She grabbed a case lying on top of the locker as she twisted her body into a rotation.

Without stopping at any point, she flowed, leaping off the top of the locker, over the heads of her shocked classmates, onto a desktop, and then a few more as she crossed the room without touching the ground.

She had shot with all the force of a cannon.

And now she leaped especially far off the last desk—into the group of girls sitting at the front of the class.

♂♀

Three days earlier, noon, apartment building, Shinjuku

"I suppose. I hope there's no bullying...but I very much doubt that," the information agent sighed...then grinned. "The poor things."

"That's not something to laugh about. They're your family, aren't they?" Namie said, her eyebrows tense with disgust, but Izaya only shook his head.

"Ohh no, no, no. Not that," he chuckled, then corrected, "The ones I feel sorry for aren't Kururi and Mairu...it's the kids trying to bully them."

"Huh?"

"What did I tell you? My sisters are weird because of *my* influence."

"For example...do you think the people who tried to bully me got away scot-free?"

♂♀

Back to the morning of the third day of school.

The classroom was frozen.

Every person present stood in place, eyes trembling, unable to process what they'd just seen.

*   *   *

"Ha-ha-ha! Gotcha!"

Mairu's innocent cry echoed off the walls, the voice of a child playing tag.

But her actions were actually the polar opposite of innocent.

The case she'd grabbed off the top of the locker was stuffed to the lid with pushpins.

Mairu cleverly popped it open one-handed, swinging it high overhead.

Everything she'd done to that point was quite simple.

She leaped into the midst of the girls who laughed at her, tackled the nearest one with a lariat, and plunged the flat of her hand into the girl's mouth when she started to scream in shock.

That was all.

Each and every one of those actions was as crisp as a series of slow-motion photographs to her classmates.

Mairu's pretty face went red, and she cackled excitedly as she rode the bucking girl like a horse. It might have been an erotic pose if not for the hand in the girl's mouth and the case of pushpins held in the other hand.

Mairu put on the exact same smile she wore during her introduction on the first day of school, her eyes glittering behind her glasses.

"I'll give you three seconds! *Who did it?* Point them out," she said, bringing the case of pushpins closer to her victim's open mouth.

"Nnnng! Nnah! Mmaaaeegh!"

The girl struggled mightily, realizing what would happen to her, but Mairu pinned her down with a knee on either shoulder, preventing her from moving on her own.

The girls in the group around them were blank with uncomprehending disbelief. They writhed uncomfortably, but otherwise did nothing.

"Three..."

The stunning precision of the assault completely robbed the wits and agency of the girl who had been the perpetrator of the bullying and was now the victim of this violence.

"Two..."

She didn't have the time to think about what would happen to her if she sold out the one who came up with the idea. Then again, if she had the time to calmly weigh the two choices of punishment later or the present threat of pushpins poured down her throat, she might have chosen the same thing anyway.

"One..."

The case of pins tilted slightly, causing them to slide and shuffle just a bit.

That sound was what did it.

The girl pointed out the tallest of her companions, who had just been gleefully discussing the result of their desk defacement moments ago.

"Zer... Ooh, close one! Thanks."

Mairu pulled her other hand out of the girl's mouth and deftly snatched the few pins that fell out before they landed. She stood up with a brilliant smile, then turned to the classmate that the nearly unconscious and terrified girl had pointed out.

The ringleader was already attempting to flee the scene when Mairu saw her.

"Oh no, you don't! You're not getting away!"

No sooner were the words out of her mouth than Mairu was hurling the few pushpins that had fallen into her hand with a motion like a pitching machine at a batting cage.

Tak-tak echoed a rhythmic sound throughout the room.

Several pins were stuck into the door that the tall girl was reaching for in her escape attempt. This in itself wasn't that abnormal; a pin could stick into the wall like a dart if it was thrown right.

But the act of hurling pushpins itself *was* abnormal, especially at a person. But Mairu Orihara broke that taboo without a second thought, tossing them right at the hand of the ringleader bully.

When she realized this, the girl stopped still for a moment out of sheer terror. She was on her heels. Every action was merely a reaction.

The ringleader had leaped into action first but was now thrust into reaction. She didn't have time to think about her next move or even act on instinct. The very target of her bullying grabbed her shoulder from behind.

"Let's go have a chat in the bathroom! Guess what! Listen! Guess what! You know what? I don't even know your name, but now I want to be *really, really good friends* with you! Ha-ha-ha!"

*   *   *

And with a playful smile on her attractive features, Mairu Orihara dragged the unidentified girl down the hallway by her chin.

She stopped for just an instant to tell the boy who sat next to her, "Sorry about this! I'll treat you to lunch later if you clean off my desk!"

The boy flinched in surprise, but not having any better idea of what to do, he went ahead and started to erase the permanent ink with his eraser.

None of the other students moved. The only sound in the class was the scraping of the eraser against the surface of the desk.

A boy who attended the same middle school as the Orihara twins arrived at school immediately afterward, and seeing the state of Mairu's desk and the terrified students, he put the pieces together. He sighed and muttered, "Oh boy, you went and did it, didn't you?"

The boy walked into the midst of the petrified students and explained, "She goes to some kind of weird martial arts gym, so I wouldn't mess with her. The few guys who tried to gang up on her a while back got beaten half to death by the other gym people."

Does this fighting style use pushpins as a weapon? everyone wanted to ask but decided that discretion was the better part of valor.

Fifteen minutes later, as homeroom was just about to start, Mairu returned to the class as though nothing had happened, straightening her clothes out. When she saw the poor male student who was still rubbing away at her desk, she bowed apologetically.

"Oh, sorry, sorry! It's oil based, so it won't come out easily, I bet. I'll help!"

She pulled a piece of cloth out of the chest pocket of her black uniform and began to wipe with the boy.

"It won't come out. And I suppose water won't work on permanent ink… Would it be faster to shave it off with a plane?" she laughed.

If you only looked at her face, she was a pretty, tidy, nerdy-looking girl. But when the boy realized he was staring at her, he quickly looked down and subsequently noticed something odd.

The cloth she was using to wipe the desk was trailing what looked like a string. It seemed strange to him, but he went back to focusing on his own work rather than get distracted.

Which meant that he failed to realize that it was the bra of the female student who'd just been dragged to the bathroom.

In the end, the girl who was primarily responsible for scribbling on Mairu's desk did not return to the classroom. She left school early without even retrieving her bag.

There was no way for anyone else to know what kind of "discussion" the two had in the bathroom—and no one was inclined to find out, either.

The students who had silently watched the defacement happen certainly weren't going to stick their necks into even bigger trouble. That was the only reason they needed.

♂♀

Time passed, and then it was homeroom before the end of school.

As a result of Mairu Orihara's rampage in Class 1-B, the twisted network of female gossip set its sights instead on Kururi Orihara, her sister.

Aoba considered the desk graffiti in silence.

She had done nothing. Kururi became the target of harassment for no other reason than being Mairu's sister. They didn't hate Kururi, they just wanted revenge against Mairu.

Actually, I don't really care, he thought, looking out of the window in boredom as time ticked down to the start of homeroom.

The teacher showed up and began to run through the standard procedures before the end of school. As Mr. Marumura looked dutifully over the entire class, he noticed the miserable state of Kururi's desk and asked, "Orihara, what happened to your desk?"

"..."

"Just to be sure...you didn't write this yourself, did you?"

He looked down and saw the content of the messages and grimaced as he waited for her answer.

"...No," the girl in the gym clothes claimed in a quiet voice.

Marumura surveyed the classroom and asked, "Does anyone know who wrote this?"

I don't care, Aoba thought, as he watched Kururi stare downward at the desk. He had nothing to do with this bullying. It represented neither benefit nor harm to him.

I really don't care.

And because he truly didn't care…

"Tsukiyama and a girl from another class did it," Aoba said, simply answering the teacher's question with the truth. Because he *didn't care.* He had no opinion either way on the bullying. He just answered the question.

Meanwhile, the girl named Tsukiyama whom he accused looked shocked. No one had stopped her when they were doing the deed. So it never occurred to her that she might be betrayed in this way.

Of course, in reality, there was no cooperation in the deed from the start, so there was nothing to betray, but from her perspective, she had been stabbed in the back.

"Come to the faculty room after this, Tsukiyama. And bring your friend from the other class. Got that?" the teacher ordered sternly.

Tsukiyama ground her teeth and shot Aoba a look that said, *You didn't do anything earlier. You just watched!* But as he didn't care, this meant nothing to him.

The one thing that he *did* care about was that Kururi herself looked at him with some amount of surprise. He couldn't deny his interest in that.

♂♀

After school, school entrance

Several hours after that incident…

"After school tomorrow…I can't wait."

Once Aoba had finished observing the various school clubs, he got a message from Mikado agreeing to show him around Ikebukuro the following afternoon.

He was heading for the school entrance to leave for the day when a fierce voice called out, "Hey, you."

Aoba turned back to see a group of girls. They were from his class, and standing at the center was Tsukiyama, the girl he'd sent to the faculty room earlier.

"What?" he asked.

Tsukiyama scowled. "You know what. What do you think you're doing?"

"Are you going to ask me out? Is that what this is? Well, sorry. I don't think I'm up to the task of going out with all of you at once," he commented lightly, but the girls did not find that amusing.

"Huh? Are you an idiot or something? Try to take a damn hint. Who snitches to the teacher in that situation? You think you're some kind of hotshot, playing the hero like that?"

"Actually, if I thought I was doing the right thing, I would have stopped you when you were doing it, right? Why would you ask me this?"

"Then why did you snitch on me?!"

"Well, you didn't tell me not to. To be honest, if I had to judge you and Orihara on a scale—based only on your looks and actions, since that's all I have to work with—I'd say it's pretty much a law of nature that a girl who draws nasty messages on someone's desk is less desirable than a mysterious, well-behaved girl with a big rack in tight gym clothes…"

"Fuck you, you little—"

Just as the girls began to close in on Aoba, Tsukiyama noticed something wrong.

Her body was sending abrupt danger signals, centering around her nostrils.

Something smelled *charred*.

"Huh…?"

A fire?

The girl looked around in a panic, searching for the source of the burning smell. It was Aoba who pinpointed the location of the smell first.

"Hey, is that…?"

"Huh? Aaagh!!"

Tsukiyama looked down to see that smoke was issuing from the bag slung over her shoulder. She screamed and threw it aside. Instantly, flames erupted from it, the smoke pouring from the burned hole in the fabric.

The smoke alarm set into the ceiling of the school's front entrance went off, ringing all throughout the school.

After that, every student present, including Aoba, was summoned to the disciplinary room for individual questioning.

Aoba answered truthfully about everything he'd seen. Oddly enough, they asked to see the contents of his bag. Surprised that they would demand this, he asked what the cause of the fire was. The teacher wouldn't tell him at first, then admitted the answer as long as he didn't tell anyone else.

They didn't know what caused the fire in Tsukiyama's bag to start, but the investigation turned up several energy drink bottles that were actually full of paint thinner. And not only that, but the bags of the other girls present led to more bottles of thinner. They denied any knowledge of this, but they'd also just been disciplined for bullying.

"Huffing paint right on the first week of school… Then again, these are bullies we're talking about. They were bothering you about what happened at homeroom, weren't they?"

"Pretty much."

"Well, they could be looking at a suspension…but there's no telling how they might try to get back at you. If things are seeming dicey, come and tell me at once."

After that, Aoba was unceremoniously released, and he headed for the school exit again—but there were two girls waiting at the front entrance this time, which still contained a bit of ash from the burned bag.

One was Kururi, carrying her bag and still in gym clothes, and the other was dressed almost the exact opposite—yet aside from the glasses, they had the exact same facial features.

"Heya. Hi! Or should it be 'good evening'? And between you and me, I guess it's 'nice to meet you'! I'm Mairu Orihara! Kuru's twin sister! It's a pleasure!"

The other girl was as bright and chatty as her sister was silent and somber.

"Um, n-nice to meet you."

They sure are odd twins, Aoba thought. Kururi, who was standing in Mairu's shadow, mumbled toward the ground, "…Thank you"

"Huh? …Oh, for the thing at homeroom? You're mistaken. I didn't do it to earn your thanks, and I didn't stop them from writing on your desk in the first place."

"…I know."

"Hweh?" he mumbled.

Mairu cackled and added, "You know that Kuru was secretly watching them do that from the hallway, right? And you know that the both of us were secretly watching the whole scene that happened here earlier?"

"What?!" Aoba stammered, shocked at this revelation. "But... wouldn't that give you even less of a reason to thank me?"

"Kuru's happy that you said you thought she was cuter than that Tsukiyama girl! You know how she's more of the silent, thoughtful type, yet she wears those gym clothes all the time? Kinda weird, right? So she's just happy that a boy actually said that about her!"

"...Be quiet," Kururi commanded her little sister. She took a step closer to Aoba, still facing downward. She and the boy were about the same height.

She said, "...Your reward."

And she looked up at last, leaned forward, and covered Aoba's lips with her own.

——?!

Not realizing at first what had just happened, Aoba's mind was a total blank. He only watched as Kururi shuffled away, her face red.

But that wasn't the end of his confusion. Mairu stepped forward to take the place of the retreating Kururi, and unlike her sister, she forcefully grabbed his body and yanked him toward her for a powerful kiss.

——?! ——?! ?! ?!

With Aoba's childish looks, it could have easily been a role reversal of man and woman. His mind went from recovering its wits to losing them again. He stared at her in blank shock. Mairu pulled back and, without missing a beat, declared, "Yippee! I shared an indirect kiss with Kuru! Hee-hee-hee!"

She hopped away from Aoba and continued in the same tone of voice, "Sorry about that. It's probably a big shock to receive that from a girl who isn't your girlfriend. Then again, Kuru looks like the reserved type, but she's actually a lot more assertive than I am!"

"...Not true."

The younger of the twins ignored the elder and approached Aoba, giggling as she leaned in for a very long whisper.

"Oh, but even if you fall in love with Kuru, you can't monopolize her! She belongs to me, too, you know! Also, I've decided that the only man for me is Yuuhei Hanejima! In fact, Kuru's a big Yuuhei Hanejima fan, too, so you might not get anything more than that kiss from her! Ha-ha-ha!"

"But Yuuhei Hanejima is…a huge star."

"Yeah, I know. Why do you mention it?"

"Never mind…um…huh? What am I supposed to do about this?"

Aoba was much too confused by the series of events for this to work as the dating sim development it could have been. Once he collected his breath and thoughts, he asked a question that had nothing to do with their kisses.

"Umm…oh, right. Did you put something in those girls' bags? Tsukiyama and them, I mean. Like…stuff."

It was a very direct and pointed question—which the girl who had kissed him on the third day they met, without any romantic connection, answered in a tiny voice.

"…That's a secret."

With a shy little smile at the end.

After the twins left, Aoba stayed there for a while, leaning against the shoe locker at the front entrance. Eventually, he remembered something and brought up a friend's number on his phone.

"Yeah, hello? It's me…"

"I feel like I just turned into the protagonist of a really bad porno."

"Would you believe me if I said that I just got kissed out of the blue by a pair of twins?"

"Huh? Yeah, they're cute. Kinda weird, but in terms of their facial features, they're pretty cute."

"Kill me? Why? No, I just figured that I would ask whether I should be happy or freaked out, from the perspective of a loser like you… Okay, sorry, that one's my fault. Don't scrape the phone speaker against the glass—aaaaagh! Stop it!"

♂♀

That night, Ikebukuro

"I don't see it, Kuru. I'm pretty sure that glider was going in this direction, though. Aww, geez. I just wanna see it, I wanna see it, I wanna!"

Mairu was shouting and carrying on, her kiss with an unfamiliar boy earlier in the afternoon completely forgotten. They were both in their own clothes now, but their fashion sense was odd nonetheless. Their affect was different from during the daytime.

"..."

Kururi, meanwhile, scanned the area in silence.

After going home from school, they leaped all over the live footage of the Black Rider and rushed out into the city to catch sight of it.

There was still heavy foot traffic in the shopping district, but as it was a normal weekday, once you got off the beaten path, it quickly turned quiet.

As they headed down one such lonely street, Mairu asked her older sister, "By the way, why are we coming this way? Shouldn't we look on one of the bigger streets?"

Kururi ignored her and continued to look around, eventually settling on a car parked on the street. She began walking straight toward it.

"...This way."

No sooner had she said it than Kururi crouched down and reached under the car.

"Whoa, what are you doing, Kuru? Did you find a ten-yen coin? Yippee! You can buy me one of those cheapo puffed corn snacks! I'll take the *mentaiko* flavor, please!" Mairu teased, cackling. But her sister got back to her feet, holding what she'd found under the car.

"What's that?" Mairu asked. Her sister didn't ignore her this time.

"...I saw...the Black Rider...drop it...on TV."

"Huh? No way, it dropped something? I didn't notice!" Mairu exclaimed in surprise. She examined the object her sister found with great interest.

Then she said...

"What's up with this *envelope*?"

*   *   *

It was a brown manila envelope with "Payment—Celty Sturluson" written on it in Japanese.

The envelope was surprisingly heavy and felt as though it contained a stack of paper. Kururi was already anticipating the answer before she opened it up.

As soon as she saw what was inside, her eyes went wide, and she glanced around.

"What's up, Kuru?"

At the very instant that the younger sister got her own peek into the envelope, something writhed in the corners of their vision. They both spun around to see.

Ikebukuro at night. In the middle of an empty street.

A monster stood there, ready to silence the girls in the lonely midst of the city.

It was tall, with exceedingly pale skin. And it appeared to be wandering about aimlessly.

But its face was hideously twisted from the nose outward, with bright-red blood spilling from eyes, ears, nose, and mouth as it shuffled forward with zombielike steps.

"…What's that?"

"Stay back, Kuru."

Mairu determined that this represented a threat, and she stood in front of her sister, right in the path of the obviously dangerous figure.

And just when he was mere inches away from entering Mairu's roundhouse kick range, the bloodied man fell over, muttering something.

"…? What's up with him? Should we call an ambulance?" the girl wondered. Right then, the man's head rose, and he spoke in halting, trembling Japanese.

"Hospital…not so…good… Miss…is there…*gahfk!*"

"…Yo-u okay?"

There was blood in the man's cough. He slowly rolled to face upward again and just barely managed to mumble, "I'm sorry… It might not be possible…but before I die…I need to do one…thing…"

"What, what? This is really interesting. Can you tell me?"

*   *   *

"Are you aware…of any sushi shops…run by Russians…around here…?"

♂♀

Ten minutes later, Sunshine, Sixtieth Floor Street, Ikebukuro

With a new briefcase purchased at the discount shop, Shizuo boldly strode through the night.

"What do you suppose that thief was all about, Tom?"

"Don't ask me, man," Shizuo's boss answered lazily. He thought about the event earlier in the evening. "I guess we could check back there later. Don't want to get in trouble if it turns out that white guy died."

"You realize he was trying to starve us by stealing our stuff, right? He must have known there was the possibility of being killed."

"Y'know, sometimes you can say the most aggressive things…," Tom muttered, feeling a cold sweat run down his back. He determined that further comments might result in his own bodily harm, so he set about checking their next collection point with a sigh.

When he wasn't pissed, Shizuo was a fairly quiet man. Right now he was somewhere in between. He probably wasn't fully over the bizarre and uncalled-for attempted robbery (?) from before.

They decided they ought to grab a bite to eat before they headed to their next job and were looking for a suitable destination when they heard a pleased shout.

"Shii-zuu-oo!"

A girl leaped onto Shizuo's back.

"…"

He reacted with something resembling a wry smile. Whatever it was, it wasn't good.

Shizuo reached around his back and picked up the girl by the collar like a kitten.

"Oh no, no, no, it'll stretch! You're stretching my clothes, Shizuo!"

"Mairu…what the hell are you doing out here in the middle of the night?"

He dangled her out in front of him, confirming that it was indeed the little sister of the man he hated more than anyone else in the world.

"To see you, of course!"

"I know you're only after Kasuka..."

"Yeah! But I love you, too, Shizuo. You're so strong!"

"...Whatever. Even I don't have access to Kasuka's schedule anymore. He's a big star now, I hear." Shizuo grunted exasperatedly, lowering Mairu to the ground. He looked over and saw Kururi watching from a distance. The girl bowed shyly.

"...For a second, I was worried you were gonna snap there, man." Tom grinned nervously, his face twitching slightly.

Shizuo scratched his head and said, "Well...I don't usually snap on people who are at least honest and straightforward about it."

What Shizuo Heiwajima hated was people who used logic to twist others around and stir up their emotions. First and foremost of this type was Izaya Orihara, and while his sisters were also insane, they were more honestly so, and therefore he didn't get as angry with them.

Naturally, he didn't put up with everything they did—but given their obvious admiration for him, Shizuo did not display any open antagonism toward them.

He did, however, show some irritation at the inevitable thought of their brother. "Listen, if your brother dies laughing as he gets shoved into a dump truck, I might just introduce you to my brother. In fact, I'm kinda frustrated today, so maybe I'll blow off steam by beating Izaya to death."

"If Iza will do the trick, then go right ahead!" Mairu suggested, selling her brother into certain death. Shizuo sighed again.

Nearby, Tom thought that it was quite rare for Shizuo to sigh like a normal person, but he chose to keep that observation to himself.

"Oh, right! I want to talk more with you, but there's a specific reason I came over, Shizuo!"

"What?"

"Listen, listen. Iza took us to this sushi place run by Russians around here. Do you know where it is? We got lost looking for it..."

"Oh, Simon's place? And don't call him Iza. Call him Fleabrains from now on."

It struck Shizuo as an odd request, but he gave them thorough directions to their destination (which was actually just a single corner away).

Meanwhile, Tom noticed the other, much shyer girl and thought, *Shizuo and a withdrawn teenage girl… Can't tell if they're totally unsuited for each other or just the opposite.* But when he saw the envelope in her hands, his eyes went wide.

Inside the opened envelope was a stack of Yukichi Fukuzawas—about a hundred of them. He looked around carefully, approached the girl, and whispered, "Hey, you shouldn't be carrying those around in the envelope."

"…!"

As she hastily closed the envelope, he handed her the paper bag that had contained the clock he just bought at the discount shop. "It's better than nothing. And make sure you don't drop it."

"…Thank you"

"It's fine. I was just looking for a place to throw the bag away."

Finished with the directions, Mairu came back to grab Kururi's hand and drag her away.

"Thank you, Shizuo!"

"…See you. Say hi…to Kasuka."

Tom watched the two girls race off and sighed.

Still just in their first or second year at Raira…and they've made a huge stack of cash like that… How long did it take them to earn that, and what did they have to give up?

After a while, he turned to Shizuo and mumbled, "I know they say that kids these days are liberal when it comes to sex…but money can be a scary thing."

"?"

"Then again…we collect debts for a hookup service, so I guess we're not in any position to lecture…"

Tom nodded to himself, pitying the plight of the young women without realizing that he was completely wrong about it. Shizuo watched his boss, and after the meeting with Mairu, he thought about his younger brother.

Oh yeah. He said he was on location in Ikebukuro today.

We live in the same neighborhood. You'd think he could drop me a line once in a while.

Chat room

TarouTanaka: At any rate, tomorrow I'll be around Ikebukuro, guiding and being guided.
TarouTanaka: I'm still a newcomer to this city, so it's good to meet you.
Kuru: That is a coincidence. We, too, have plans to travel through Ikebukuro tomorrow. Perhaps we might even meet face-to-face and fist-to-fist.
Mai: We're gonna punch 'em?
TarouTanaka: If we do, go easy on me, lol.
Kuru: Our trip out this evening was quite wonderful. Are you aware of the sushi place known as Russia Sushi? That is a most fascinating establishment.
Mai: Yummy.
TarouTanaka: Oh! I know it! Russia Sushi! That's where Simon works!
Bacura: The employees are scary, though.
Kuru: Oh, what a detailed response... Perhaps we have passed by each other on the streets already. Just outside Russia Sushi maybe.
Mai: Near miss.
TarouTanaka: Oh, I go to the bowling alley right next door all the time.
Bacura: And I went to the Taiwanese restaurant on the third floor and the arcade on the second floor pretty often.
Saika: everyone knows so much.
TarouTanaka: Well, out of all of us, I bet Kanra knows the most about this place.

Kanra has entered the chat.

Kanra: Yoo-hoo, everyone!
Kanra: Oh, we have some newcomers.
TarouTanaka: Good evening.
Kuru: It has been quite a while, Kanra. To think that our reunion would take place not in the flesh, but the cybernetic world! The Internet can make the distance between people shrink or grow... A truly futuristic tool, in my opinion.

Mai: Long time no see.
Bacura: Evenin'.
Kanra: Umm…hang on a sec.

<Private Mode> Kanra: Is that you, Kururi and Mairu?
<Private Mode> Kanra: How'd you get the address to this chat?!
<Private Mode> Kuru: Miss Namie thoughtfully told us, Brother Izaya.
<Private Mode> Kanra: …So she already made contact with you…?
<Private Mode> Kanra: Listen to me. Just leave for today.
<Private Mode> Kanra: There are lots of things I need to tell you about later.
<Private Mode> Kuru: I understand, Brother. I look forward to hearing your voice in person.

Mai: Okay, I'm leaving.
TarouTanaka: ?

<Private Mode> Kanra: Use private mode! Whatever, just log off!

Kuru: Kanra says that he hates us, so we are going to leave.
Kanra: Hey, come on, that's a little harsh for a joke! ☆
Kuru: I will pray that the next time we meet, Kanra's mood has improved.
Saika: fighting is bad
Mai: I'm sorry.
Kanra: Aah! It was a joke! You don't have to take it so seriously!
Kuru: Well, have a good one, everyone.
Mai: Buh-byes.
TarouTanaka: Oh, good night.

Kuru has left the chat.
Mai has left the chat.

Bacura: Good night. What's with the "buh-byes" at the end? lol
Saika: good night

Kanra: Enough of that! Let's regroup and start anew!

TarouTanaka: So, um, who were they after all?

Kanra: Pay them no mind or you'll die!

TarouTanaka: It causes death?!

Kanra: Just forget it! So anyway...

Kanra: Hiya, it's me, Kanra!

TarouTanaka: Hello again.

Bacura: 'Sup.

Saika: good evening. it is a pleasure again today.

Kanra: Sure thing. ☆ Is everyone used to the new chat system by now?

TarouTanaka: Yes, the different colors for each person makes it easy to identify who's who.

Bacura: Indeed,

Bacura: This allows us to gang up on Kanra more vividly than ever.

Kanra: Vividly?! Oh no, what are you going to do to little old me?!

Bacura: An endless repetition of beatings and neglect.

.

.

.

The next day, Ikebukuro

It was a sunny afternoon. Raira Academy uniforms could be spotted here and there throughout the neighborhood.

The first-year students were done with class earlier than second- or third-years, so it was they who were out on the town now.

Kururi and Mairu were walking down the sidewalk next to Sunshine City. They appeared to be walking with purpose—but for whatever reason, Mairu's footsteps were heavy. It was as if the soles of her feet were sending roots into the earth, and for this one moment, her face was actually gloomier than Kururi's.

"...Cheer up."

"Ugh...I'm sorry, Kuru, I'm sorry... But it's such a terrible shock..."

Mairu was holding a tabloid paper in her hand.

On the front it read "Yuuhei Hanejima and Ruri Hijiribe in a Late-Night Tryst?!," complete with an article describing the discovery of a meeting between Mairu's beloved Yuuhei Hanejima and megastar singer Ruri Hijiribe in the middle of the night.

"Yuuhei... Yuuhei's going to belong to someone else... Oh, if only this Ruri was Kururi instead, then I could bear it. I'd be delighted, in fact! So why, why?! My heart is being torn to pieces! The value of my sadness is equal to Graham's number!"

Graham's number was the greatest "meaningful number," according to the *Guinness Book of World Records*, an amount so vast that anyone who wasn't well versed in mathematics would quickly overheat in the attempt to comprehend it.

Her sister might not have understood the significance of that, but she did recognize Mairu's shock. Kururi curled around in the center of the sidewalk and sealed her little sister's lips shut with her own.

"Mm...!"

Just like Aoba yesterday, Mairu's eyes widened in surprise.

Two teenage girls locked in a passionate kiss right on the street. It was a sight both tantalizingly illicit and abnormal, and if a staff writer for *Wakahime Club* had been present, he would have snapped photos with tears in his eyes.

Mairu was surprised by that unexpected action but soon took on a blissful look and clutched back at her sister's body.

As if on cue, Kururi pulled her lips away and grinned.

"...Feeling better?"

"Yeah! I feel way better! Girls' lips are so soft and wonderful! Especially yours, Kuru! Can I shout yahoo? Yahoo! One more time! One more time!" Mairu danced, writhing with stimulation.

Kururi's smile vanished. "...You're creepy."

"What?! That's messed up! It's the most messy of messed-up messes! Just after we had rekindled our love for one another! Not only that, you kiss another girl—your own sister, to boot—and then claim it's creepy? What's that about?! Is this a honey trap?! Are you luring me in just to criticize me?! No fair! It's like... Oh, I know! It's like you're the Road Runner, and I'm Wile E. Coyote!"

Mairu's analogy didn't make much sense. Kururi hung her head in troubled exasperation, then grinned again as she looked up.

But before she could say anything—

"Hey, heyyy! What's up, girls? Quite a show you're puttin' on!"

"I mean, two girls makin' out in the middle of the day? Crazy aggressive stunt, yeah?"

"More like aggresstunt, am I right? Hah."

"So that's hilarious and all, but can you let us get in on that tip?"

"Why do you do it between girls? It makes no sense. You do that because the guys give you no attention?"

"'Cuz we'll step in and provide!"

"But only if you can tell us where to find the Black Rider."

From somewhere inconspicuous, where they had noticed the rather attention-grabbing stunt of girls' kissing, emerged a group of very *conspicuous* men dressed in striped motorcycle gang outfits.

And as a result, the girls, too, were dragged into Ikebukuro's holiday.

CHAPTER 4
GAO MAGAZINE SPECIAL ARTICLE "SPOTTED! YUUHEI HANEJIMA AND RURI HIJIRIBE IN A LATE-NIGHT TRYST?!"

Roots Smile Café, Higashi-Nakano

In a bar fairly close to Higashi-Nakano Station, with walls lined with various bottles of liquor and a pleasant handmade quality to the furnishings, a number of young people bustled, the sound of their merriment a kind of BGM for the establishment.

At a table in the very back sat two men, facing each other. One of them nervously glanced around, while the other drank a virgin cocktail, his face completely expressionless.

The emotionless man drained his glass, his eyes as cold as ice. When he was done, he ordered another from the bartender, still without a hint of feeling.

He turned to the older man sitting across from him and flatly asked, "Aren't you going to have a drink, Mr. Kanemoto?"

"I have to go back to the office and work after this," the restless Kanemoto said politely to the younger man. His table partner had a face so smooth and delicate, he could have passed as a boy—or even a woman. His features were handsome and striking, the very manifestation of beauty in the flesh.

His hair was a combination of countless perfect silky strands, as smooth and flowing as a river, perfectly jet-black and softly feminine.

At a glance, he looked like a prince out of a girls' manga, but there was a chilly personality emanating from him that made him far from welcoming.

Eventually, an order of pasta reached the table, and the young man said in a monotone, "Go ahead, Mr. Kanemoto."

"N-no, you first, Mr. Yuuhei," he said, appending a polite title to the younger man's name. Yuuhei picked up his fork without another word.

It was pasta alla carbonara, the chewy-looking noodles topped with rich cream sauce and fragrant bacon. The young man nimbly rolled his fork until he had accumulated a wad of pasta the size of a golf ball, which he popped into his mouth.

He chewed, carefully and silently, his face a sculpted mask. When he was done, he said, "This is good carbonara."

The other man slumped and reluctantly grabbed his own fork. "There's no way for me to tell if you're telling the truth or not, based on your expression... Oh, what do you know? It is good."

In comparison to the other man's lack of emotion, the manager began to eagerly shovel the pasta into his face. He complained, "You know this is right in front of the office, don't you? I mean...we could have a meeting at a club or someplace else. We'll pick up the tab. Why here?"

"Because it's close."

"Oh, I see... So you're saying...you *don't* have any interest in visiting a club?"

"I don't know. I've never considered it. I'll look into it if I get the chance," the young man said.

Kanemoto sighed and continued with business. "Well, in that case... are you up on tomorrow's schedule?"

"I have an interview at a hotel in Ikebukuro at six thirty, and then I'm going home."

"...Yes, that's right."

The conversation paused again. It wasn't that the young man refused to speak, he just didn't show any emotion when he did so. Because of that, Kanemoto was unsure of how to proceed or if what he was saying was displeasing his conversation partner.

"..."

"It's very good."

"...I know. I already finished mine... At any rate, tomorrow's interview is promotion for the movie, so keep that in mind."

"Okay."

Yuuhei nodded and continued to eat his meal like an animatronic figure. His professional manager Kanemoto looked at the young man and thought, *I only took on this job because Uzuki asked me to... He's not acting this way because he hates me, is he?*

"Um, well...in that case, let's just get through the next three days, while Uzuki's off on his honeymoon..."

"Yes, of course," Yuuhei responded, still cold and mechanical. Kanemoto bowed again.

He had to avoid any displays of rudeness. The attractive young man sitting before him was worth millions—possibly billions—of yen. He was a bona fide money tree.

♂♀

From the Internet encyclopedia Fuguruma Youki

An except from the "Yuuhei Hanejima" article

Yuuhei Hanejima—an actor and model. Born in Toshima Ward of Tokyo.

His birth date is unclear, as the president of Jack-o'-Lantern Japan, Max Sandshelt, has claimed on different occasions that he is "a cyborg born in the year 3258," and "a vampire that's been alive for over a millennium," and "a warrior of light from the ancient continent of Atlantis who was never reincarnated." Calculations from his appearance at the coming-of-age ceremonial holiday estimate that he is just around twenty-one years old.

His real name is Kasuka Heiwajima. As stated earlier, his talent agency is Jack-o'-Lantern Japan.

In addition to his parents, his family includes an older brother. He seems to respect his brother and mentions him often in interviews. No other details about his brother are known. There is a record of a bizarre incident involving a particularly persistent journalist's car being suddenly flipped over after questioning too closely about Hanejima's family, but the connection between the two things is not certain.

What is known is that his brother is a terrifying individual. He once beat a talent scout half to death, and Hanejima's rescue of the scout was what led to his show business debut.

After modeling for a number of magazines, his first acting role was Carmilla Saizou, the lead character of the direct-to-video movie *Vampire Ninja Carmilla Saizou*. He earned cult attention for his good looks and frighteningly polished acting, and his name spread in certain circles on the Internet.

The next year, Daioh TV's flagship program *Money Gamer* ran a segment titled "How Much Can You Make in One Month with a Million Yen?" in which Yuuhei used various connections and means to reach a total of 1.2 billion yen, an incident that led to nationwide news before it even aired.

Because the rules of the segment stated that any profit from the experiment went back to the contestant, he was soon known to the public as the extraordinarily lucky boy who won himself a cool 1,199 million yen.

Yuuhei's reputation as a nouveau riche took the backseat when he exhibited his acting skill in a series of television dramas. His versatility in a variety of roles, combined with his appearance, launched him to stardom.

He is skilled at singing and athletics as well, not just acting. On top of that, his repertoire covers roles from singers to assassins, from cross-dressing to passionate bed scenes. He is known as an actor's actor.

However, outside of acting, he eliminates virtually all emotion, carrying out conversations like a flat-voiced robot. This makes him an ill fit for talk shows, but many of his fans find this to be cool, and he is therefore known as naturally expressionless. In his words, "I used to cry and laugh as a kid, but I learned by the example of my brother, who had extreme emotional swings, and that's why I act like this. But I still deeply respect him."

In one nonfaked hidden-camera prank segment, Yuuhei was accosted by "yakuza" actors, who threatened to cut off his pinkie finger, but he showed no fear and did not resist. Right as they were about to sever his finger with a knife, the program staff had to intervene and cancel the segment.

In another incident, a stalker gave him a silent cold call on a day off, and he stayed on the line for twenty hours, until the stalker gave up. (This is only known because the silent pressure was too much to bear, disintegrating the stalker's will and causing her to turn herself in to the police.)

This mechanical personality does not endear him to others, and he has virtually no close friends in show business. For this reason, his private life is shrouded in mystery, and the interior of his home has never been filmed.

He owns a number of cars, most notably some foreign sports cars and luxury models like Mitsuoka's Le-Seyde and Galue, and he recently expressed a desire to own the Mitsuoka Orochi in a TV interview.

Because he chooses his purchases on taste with no thought for price, it is not uncommon for him to wear a cheap accessory from a one hundred–yen shop and an ultrafine million-yen accessory at the same time. He does not seem to find this odd at all. [citation needed]

Due to his ability to seemingly do anything perfectly, he has the Internet nickname "Secret-Shame Curator." This is because he is considered "a character so perfect, he's the kind of secret shame that you create in middle school and try to forget about when you grow up."

When the agency president heard about this, he said, "Then we need to make him even more perfect" and whipped up a poster with angel wings, devil horns, and nonmatching color contacts. He managed to get this image on the cover of a niche magazine, but it looked so good on him that it only made him more popular. Inexplicably, the poster also went viral overseas.

Yuuhei kept a blank expression throughout the photo shoot, but afraid of the rumors that he was "only pretending to be blank to hide his incredible rage," Max Sandshelt supposedly went back to America for two weeks for his own safety—an anecdote that aptly describes the eeriness of his icy expression.

*   *   *

After he had achieved both fame and fortune, Yuuhei stunned the showbiz world when he accepted an offer to film a sequel to *Vampire Ninja Carmilla Saizou*, a work that everyone assumed was his *own* secret shame.

When a celebrity magazine ranked him third on their list of "Actors Who Never Say No," he responded with, "Carmilla Saizou is a very respectable character. He's a wonderful ninja who knows the true meaning of love," in his usual deadpan, leaving everyone else unsure of whether he meant it or not.

He was tabbed by Hollywood director John Drox to play the lead in his pet project *Cruiserfield*, which films in Japan this spring, leading to increased interest abroad.

♂♀

And this soon-to-be Hollywood star was causing Kanemoto to come down with ulcers.

A man named Uzuki had been Yuuhei's manager since his debut, but for these three days, Kanemoto was tabbed to take over as a substitute manager while Uzuki was on his honeymoon.

I didn't think he really acted like a robot all the time.

Kanemoto had always assumed that Yuuhei's iron mask was just another act he put on for the TV cameras. Anyone who saw his effortless swing of emotions when he was in character would naturally assume that this blank-faced automaton was the true act.

But this young man was anything but natural.

"Well, I'll be going, then," Yuuhei said in front of the Jack-o'-Lantern Japan building after their meal, as he got into his car.

Today he was driving a Ferrari. Kanemoto didn't know much about the specific model, but he could recognize that it was a Ferrari from the red color, distinct body, and horse logo.

In the passenger seat was a plastic bag from a convenience store carrying a beef bowl inside it, probably for a late-night meal.

A guy with eight luxury cars, buying a cheapo mini-mart beef bowl,

Kanemoto marveled as he watched the younger man drive off. He felt like he was watching a hermit in person.

Yuuhei Hanejima was the agency's diamond, a jewel that shone brighter the more it was polished. As such, Kanemoto was filled to his core by a desire not to see him damaged. Yuuhei himself might be indifferent to his own worth, but his sheer talent in every regard helped him fend for himself.

Kanemoto understood this, but he couldn't deny the overwhelming pressure not to have that diamond tarnished while it was briefly in his care. He was sick with envy at his newly married coworker in more ways than one.

But to his great misfortune, that very jewel would be dragged into Ikebukuro's holiday the very next day.

♂♀

In the darkness

Everything in one's life could be compared to a story, such as a movie, or a TV show, or a novel, or a fairy tale.

In the blind darkness, she wondered what kind of B movie her life was.

When did it start?

Time itself seemed to twist and stretch. It was all she could do to keep her wits intact as she swam through a sea of vague memory.

Oh, that's right. It was in my childhood. What I always looked up to as a child.

Giant beasts on the television screen, running and flailing about as they toppled high-rise buildings and the Tokyo Tower.

They weren't exactly "animals," more like a cross between people, insects, and something that did not exist in our world. Monsters designed to inspire fear and disgust that rampaged at will, without humility or excuses.

She felt a kind of adoration of these movie monsters, the *kaiju.*

At the time, she was too young to be able to describe what drew her to those creatures with words. But now, she could.

In her innocent youth, she understood that she *could never be like them.*

Obviously, no one could be a giant monster that stood hundreds of feet tall. It wasn't in that sense.

She wanted to be something that was unfettered by anything, doing as it pleased, without regard for anyone else's opinion. Even if the result of that was destruction.

Unconsciously, she came to a realization—that she could never live outside of the law, and even on the straight and narrow path, she could not expose who she really was.

Her family was one of the richest in an already-wealthy neighborhood.

It was a "distinguished line," whatever that meant. All it amounted to was that she had to wear the mask of family and continue the act of her bloodline. Her parents, extended family, and others never explicitly said this to her, but the expectation and the atmosphere that existed before she was even born placed a powerful pressure on her instincts.

They weren't the kind of distinguished line that had political or financial connections or the ability to bend society to their will. They were just a family that happened to have earned a bunch of money at some point a few generations in the past.

It was probably this tenuous connection to dignity that caused them to be so dedicated to the pursuit of "distinguished" behavior—it was the only way they could maintain that dignity.

And now, the estate was gone.

Her grandfather's business failed, and her father got burned in the futures market trying to make up for that loss. They went bankrupt.

Her mother left the family, and her current whereabouts were unknown.

The house burned for some reason.

Several relatives with hefty debts hung themselves.

Some relatives without hefty debts hung themselves, too.

With hindsight, she could see that it wasn't the debt that was crushing to them; it was the loss of that pride and honor, the only thing they could rely upon. A true distinguished family would maintain their dignity even if they lost everything, but the nouveau riche couldn't protect or discard their pride, and the only thing left in between was despair.

As one of the few survivors, she mourned the loss of her family.

But she also gained freedom at last.

After many twists and turns being raised by distant relatives, she finally found what she wanted to do. It involved those movie *kaiju* that she admired so much as a child.

It wasn't just her respect of *kaiju*, but of horror movie killers like Jason and Freddy, emotionless creatures like the Xenomorph, and all other bringers of destruction and murder that transcended both the flesh and society of humanity that led her to enroll as an apprentice makeup artist as soon as she graduated middle school.

Now she could create the monsters she had admired so much with her own hands.

And they'll do what I couldn't...

It was at this point in her reflection on her past that she finally realized what she was doing.

Oh. This is my life, flashing before my eyes.

The serial killer Hollywood, her body flying through the air after it was pummeled by a park bench, could sense her own life's imminent end.

In the midst of that extremely compressed period of time, she shut her eyes.

How had she turned into a killer?

The flashback of her life didn't need that part.

It was a part of her past she didn't want to remember.

Still, I'm satisfied.

At the end, at the very end...I finally met a real monster.

Not a fake like me, but a true, true "monster" with monster strength.

And with the second great impact of the last few seconds, her flashback vanished, sending what remained of her wits into darkness.

♂♀

At that moment

Kasuka Heiwajima, better known as Yuuhei Hanejima, was passing by, out of either coincidence or fate.

On the way home from his interview in Ikebukuro, he nimbly drove his beloved Le-Seyde through the night streets, right under the speed limit. The interview had contained several questions about his brother, so he decided to stop by and say hello, cruising the streets looking for the familiar bartender uniform that he had given Shizuo as a gift.

When this predictably didn't work, he began to wonder if he should call, or send a text, or if it was even necessary to see him at all—when his car lights caught sight of something odd down a narrow alley.

"..."

It was the twisted sight of a human figure falling from the sky, an eyeball popped out of its socket.

The thing crashed to the asphalt and twitched once, then lay still and inert. Only the silhouette could be described as "human"; in the headlights, the skin was green and covered in crawling insects, the very figure of a zombie from a movie or video game.

Most human beings would scream at this point. But Yuuhei calmly pulled the car over to the shoulder and got out to check if the figure was living or just a mannequin.

The green skin gleamed wet and sticky in the light. There was no blood, but the figure was deadly still, clearly suffering serious medical effects.

Yuuhei considered that it could be a lifelike figure rather than a human being, but the momentary twitching earlier seemed to rule that out. It was an abnormal situation to say the least, but Yuuhei did not show a single sign of panic.

People falling out of the sky was a normal sight to Yuuhei. Usually because his brother had punched them there.

As he got out his phone to call an ambulance, Yuuhei considered another possibility.

The serial killer Hollywood.

Recalling the stories of the murderous maniac who appeared in the form of various monsters, Yuuhei began to wonder if the half-dead, half-living thing on the ground was this very person.

That didn't change his course of action, however. He took a bold step forward, then noticed that the zombie's face seemed to be peeling off.

"…"

The effect was so lifelike, it looked like nothing other than rotting skin. But beneath it, Yuuhei noticed a different color—not the red of muscle or blood, but pale, ordinary skin.

An ordinary person would likely have been too panicked by the sight to calmly notice such a detail, but this young man was not ordinary. He silently reached out for the mask.

When he saw the face that emerged from beneath it, Yuuhei stopped to think.

It was only for a few seconds, during which the young man's handsome face showed no emotion, only an eerie mechanical interest, like a cleaning robot that found a piece of dirt.

Eventually, Yuuhei lifted the mysterious zombie-costumed person into his arms and toward the passenger-side door of his car. He carefully opened the door and sat the monster into the seat.

He then returned to the driver's seat, called someone on his phone, and when he was done, quietly resumed driving away.

In the darkness

Oddly, I could tell that I was dreaming.

How had it begun?

Why did I become a murderer?

I should never have *possibly* become a monster, so how did it happen?

It's what I always wanted, so why do I feel so sick?

I wanted to vomit.

I always wanted to vomit after I killed them.

But I knew that what was truly sickening was myself for being a killer.

Even as I committed the deeds, I asked myself what I was doing.

What a disgusting person I am, feeling sick at my own actions out of regret and guilt.

And even as I did it, I couldn't stop the feeling of nausea from creeping up on my backbone.

No, no, it's not right.

A monster doesn't regret.

A monster doesn't feel sick.

A monster isn't plagued by guilt.

Some monsters in the movies were like that.

But they aren't the real monsters.

They are lovable human beings. Or not human—but humanlike.

If they could share sentiments with human beings, then somewhere, somewhere, they were meant to be loved. No matter how they look.

But I am not.

I can't be like that.

I can't be loved by anyone.

I will be a monster.

A monster that no one can fathom.

And only then can I get back at them...

No, wrong.

Wrong! Wrong! Wrong!

There's one left! Just one! And yet...

One, one, one, him, he is coming
It's him It's him kill kill must kill him   kill him
       kill   him   them no him kill
kill kill no must kill or be killed vomit he's coming don't come
stay away stay away stay away stay away no no no don't don't do n't
don't touch me don't touch me   don't touch me don't touch me
don't don't don't

"This is a surprise. She heals almost as fast as Celty and your brother."

                                *   *   *

Nooo!   Who   him   no   him?   No!

    No   then who   ggh   hyaaaaa! going to ,   die   ah

                 different   voice   no   monster

"Amazing. Maybe Celty's pulling her closer. What do you think?"

Not him   whose voice   here   where   is he   is he

   must kill   someone   I'll die   yeeek!   aaaah!

"At first the syringe wouldn't even pierce the skin. Then again, Shizuo broke my scalpel. I mean, that's incredible. There's no blade more solid and flexible than a scalpel. And he broke it… It felt like I was scraping against a metal washing board or something."

Who   answer   who

          where   he   where

               Just one   more to   go   can't end   yet hyaa!

"In fact, this isn't far off… It's kind of hard to believe it'd be a girl like this. Such a beauty in the prime of her youth."

Answer   answer   answer———

   Can't end here   no   no   I don't want

                 Help   Mother   where are you

                                       Help me

Help

                           ♂♀

And then, her eyes opened.

"Oh, she's awake. Not only is there no danger to her life, she may be able to walk again in minutes."

"Thank you very much."

"Hey, I can't turn down a request from Shizuo's little brother. I don't want him coming to blast me all the way to Mars."

Her wits still weren't in focus. Her hazy vision was able to process a milky-white ceiling.

There was some kind of conversation happening around her, but it all felt like it was happening in some distant country. But she'd have to be watching the TV to see something from a far-off land, so it gave her the illusion of receiving telepathic signals instead. Eventually, the information began to get clearer.

One of the voices was devoid of emotion, while the other was cynical and playful.

"Sorry about my brother…"

"Ha-ha, actually, I should thank you, since he's been a big help to Celty somehow. But I don't want her falling in love with Shizuo, so could you tell him not to act *too* cool if he can help it? He'll punch me if I say so. Oh, and I'm a bit thirsty, so can I have a glass of water?"

"I'll bring you one."

"Oh, thanks. And one for her…if she can drink. Well, get one anyway."

The closer man's face loomed toward her. He was a smart-looking young man with glasses. Based on his white lab coat, he appeared to be a doctor.

But the background surrounding him did not look like a hospital. Bookshelves lined the wall, and there were decorative plants of the kind found at an upscale, ultramodern restaurant.

The room was certainly stylish, but that sleek look was ruined by the hangers of drying clothes hanging in the entrance doorway. There was also a tropical fish tank, its air pump bubbling away, yet she also heard a cat meowing somewhere else in the room. The whole place had an odd combination of luxury and homey comfort.

Where am I?

She blinked her cloudy eyes, trying to bring the scene into focus.

The next moment, she noticed the dull pain coming from every inch of her body.

…!

It wasn't enough to make her scream, but she did wonder how it had taken her this long to notice such pain. She clenched her eyes against it, which the doctor-like man noticed.

"Oh, I wouldn't move around yet if I were you. I gave you a pain-killer, and you seem to heal fast—but you took injuries that would normally have you passed out from the pain," he said flippantly.

She quietly tried to keep her breathing under control. If this was a hospital, there was something very important she'd need to face—but with the circumstances so uncertain, she needed to understand her situation first.

"..."

"Are you all right? Aside from the dull impact, do you have any sharp, stabbing pains?"

"..."

She shook her head. The man in the coat smiled with relief. At the very least, the doctor here did not seem to intend her any harm. She swallowed and managed to emit a voice that was weak and pained, yet driven by strong will.

"Um...where...am I...?"

It was a delicate and beautiful voice for a girl who had been wearing a horrifying zombie mask just minutes earlier, but Shinra Kishitani, the man in white, simply shook his head in ecstatic wonder.

"Ahhh, it's *just like* your voice on TV."

"Umm..."

"Oh, pardon me. But hang on a second. Before I answer your question...please just let me enjoy the bliss of meeting someone I've always wanted to meet. Not in a romantic way. Just a few seconds, if you don't mind."

"Uh, okay...," the girl on the bed said, keeping her voice low so as not to set off the throbbing in her head.

Shinra looked relieved and theatrically thrust his arms wide before his injured patient, his voice positively brimming with bliss.

"It's a cold, cruel world out there, but I'm glad to be alive! *This* is true enchantment! Oh, once you're able to move again, may I have your autograph? Two, if possible! I know I'm a shameless fanboy, but my roommate is also a huge fan of yours!"

It was hardly the most gentlemanly thing in the world, devolving into fawning excitement in the presence of an injured patient, but the black-market doctor couldn't help but bow to his personal hero.

But this wasn't limited to just him; many men would do the same in this situation. Others might be so nervous that they could barely speak.

"Who would have ever thought that I could have this job skulking in the darkness..."

Shinra spread his arms even wider and identified his patient.

"...and eventually get the chance to treat everyone's favorite idol singer, *Ruri Hijiribe!*"

♂♀

From the Internet encyclopedia Fuguruma Youki

An excerpt from the "Ruri Hijiribe" article

A Japanese actress, celebrity, and model. Affiliated with the Yodogiri Shining Corporation talent agency.

Her birth name is the same as her stage name.

Date of birth August 8, year unknown.

She was originally an apprentice of the special-effects makeup artist Tenjin Zakuroya, then made her modeling debut after she was scouted by Yodogiri Shining Corporation.

Before her debut, she handled special-effects makeup for several domestic films, with her work on *Vampire Ninja Carmilla Saizou* being especially lauded. The World Film Village Federation listed her along with her master in their list of "100 Juiciest SFX Makeup Artists."

After that, she made her magazine debut as a model and appeared in her first minor role in a TV drama six months later, winning passionate fans with her unique nature.

Her acting is not expert level; her fans are drawn to her nature underneath. Her pale skin and delicate, melancholy features give her an unearthly beauty, which has landed her a number of roles playing gloomy, weak-willed characters.

She is rumored to be the rare "straight beauty" without the need of cosmetics, but the truth of this is unknown. It's also said that she maintains the same quiet, graceful nature when the cameras aren't rolling. In interviews, she has claimed that she's poor at interacting and has no friends or boyfriend.

Although she is supposedly sold on her looks alone, her rare qualities among celebrities means that she has no competitive rival. Her ghostly nature makes her popular with men and women alike.

She is poor at physical activity and has never appeared on televised athletic segments, such as swimming races. However, because her dark characteristics make her easy to play off of during variety programs, she is often featured on talk shows. Because she speaks so seldomly, most of her character is constructed via comments and jokes from the hosts and other comedian guests. She has mentioned her lack of physical coordination on such shows.

However, due to reports that she placed highly in track-and-field events in elementary school, it's possible that her weak and nonathletic character might be a ruse. [citation needed]

Thanks to her eerie qualities and exaggerated characteristics, she is commonly voted one of the top celebrities whom manga and anime fans would like to see wear cosplay.

♂♀

It was none other than the famous idol actress Ruri Hijiribe in the room with Shinra.

She was an unearthly presence there and not just for the reason that she had been wearing bizarre zombie makeup.

Naturally, her face had no cosmetics on it. Yet her skin was as smooth as silk, and her features were as beautiful as a portrait.

You know, if Yuuhei came right out of a girls' manga, she must be an angel from a classic painting by one of the Western masters, Shinra thought, then regretted the fact that he hadn't brought an autograph board for her to sign. *It was too sudden, I guess.*

Normally, Shinra would be cleaning the apartment while waiting for Celty to come home. Instead, his phone rang with a familiar number on the display.

The brother of an old classmate claimed he had a patient he couldn't bring to a normal doctor, so he paid that acquaintance a visit. As a result, Shinra was grateful that he made the choice to be a black-market doctor.

As Ruri Hijiribe watched the man in the white coat frolic, she wondered, *Who is this man, anyway? And this looks...just like a normal room...but it's so big.*

Based on the furnishings, it looked more like an apartment than a house. The problem was, it was much too big for that to be the case.

Oh, right. What happened to me...? That man in the bartender's outfit hit me with a bench...and then...

Her memory ended there. After that, someone brought her to this place and had this doctor-looking man care for her—at least, based on what she could tell from the way the man was excitedly blathering on.

"..."

Ruri kept her silence, putting her circumstances together in her head.

I wonder if he knows...who I am.

Clearly, he knew that she was Ruri Hijiribe. But more importantly, did he know that she was the serial killer Hollywood?

First of all, it made no sense that she wasn't taken to a hospital in an ambulance. True, it would have been a bad thing for her to be taken to a hospital and identified, but she was already in a life-or-death situation when she was found.

As her body throbbed in pain, a cat suddenly climbed up onto her stomach.

"Urgh..."

The pressure of the cat's paws made the pain much worse. Ruri tried to push it off of the blanket resting on her stomach, but when she got a good look at it, she couldn't do it.

The cat was an adorable Scottish fold with tiny flopped ears and still not fully grown. It was like a ball of fluff that was given life. The creature looked at Ruri curiously and mewed.

It was so cute that the serial killer nearly forgot her pain and all her troubles for an instant.

But another man, who had entered the room in the meantime, reached out from beside the doctor and picked up the cat.

"Stop that, Dokusonmaru. You shouldn't climb on an injured person."

"Dokusonmaru?" the man in the white coat asked.

The younger man said flatly, "His full name is Yuigadokusonmaru. It means 'Mr. Egocentric.' Isn't he cute?"

The man held out the cat, but the doctor pulled back awkwardly.

"Please, smile when you do that next time. It's scary."

"But I am smiling."

"If Dad saw you, he'd try to dissect you," the black-market doctor said in resignation as he tried to read the expression of the utterly expressionless man.

Listening to the two men talk, Ruri suddenly realized that the man with the discount T-shirt and the expensive name-brand belt was a very familiar face.

"Are you...Yuuhei...Hanejima?" she mumbled. Yuuhei turned to her without a reaction and set the cat down on the floor.

"Oh, good. You're doing better than I thought," he said without moving a single muscle aside from his lips, which made it difficult to tell if he was actually relieved at all. But given that the man shared her line of work, she knew that he was simply the type of person who never displayed his true emotions.

They had actually met on a number of occasions, but they were not friends.

In fact, when Yuuhei was shooting his debut film, *Vampire Ninja Carmilla Saizou*, it was none other than Ruri who did his prosthetic makeup.

After she began acting, they appeared together just once in a two-hour TV drama. It was a serialized police procedural, with Yuuhei playing the lead detective role, while Ruri was a simple guest as the victim's daughter. That was the closest connection they shared.

Why?

She was initially more confused than surprised by their reunion.

Why was there a coworker of sorts here in the room?

He couldn't have been sent...by him...

But she dismissed the thought.

He *doesn't have any connection to Yuuhei Hanejima.*

So why? The question floated over the actress's pretty face as Yuuhei quietly asked, "Can you drink some water?" He held out a cup, his face like a robot's.

It was the perfect setup for her to be poisoned, but Ruri took it and imbibed the water without question. A dull pain ran through her body when she sat up, but it wasn't enough to prevent her from drinking.

The doctor noted, "Her muscles were torn to shreds, but it looks like her internal organs are fine. Just in case, once she's on her feet again, she should get X-rays or an MRI. Some kinds of brain hemorrhage don't show up until later. If only I had access to Nebula's research center, I could have done those for you. Sorry."

"No, you came out in the middle of the night with no notice. Thank you so much."

"Actually, I came out way ahead in the deal—I got to look at an idol way up close. Oh, and don't tell Celty I said any of this. She's a big fan of this girl, too, so she'll be jealous, just not in the usual way," the doctor said, chuckling to himself.

Suddenly, the buzzing of a cell phone emanated from his pocket, and he snuck off to the corner of the room to quietly take the call.

The two actors didn't have much to say, so the room was suddenly plunged into silence. Eventually, Ruri couldn't stand it any longer and broke the quiet by softly asking, "Why am I here?"

"I was on my way home when you fell in front of my car. I know you didn't ask for it, but I took you home and called a doctor I know to come look at you."

"Why here, instead of a hospital?"

"Well, there are a number of reasons…"

He paused briefly and took a breath before continuing, "I thought… you might not want a hospital."

"…"

"I apologize if my decision wasn't the correct one. I can even take you to a hospital now, if you want."

"…No, it's fine."

Yuuhei was still totally flat in his affect, while Ruri remained suspicious. Their conversation was distant and polite, but it gave way to more silence.

At that point, the doctor returned, shaking his head.

"Sorry, got another emergency patient! Two in one night—who

would have thought? Damn, just when I had a chance to get to know Ruri Hijiribe," he complained. As he prepared to leave, he leaned over to Yuuhei's ear to whisper, "Think you could get me an autograph from her? One for Celty, too. Much appreciated!"

"I'll ask."

"Thanks! As a sign of my appreciation, today's visit is free of charge!"

"No, I can't…"

"I insist! I'll just charge my next patient out the wazoo for the crime of cutting my time here short! Say hi to Shizuo for me!"

Still smiling, the man in the white doctor's coat left the room.

The cat followed the other man out of the room, as if seeing him to the door, leaving only two megastars behind.

But here there were no adoring fans, only silence and the fruitless passage of time.

This time, it was Yuuhei, sitting in the chair at the side of the bed, who broke the silence.

"May I ask something?"

"…What is it?" Ruri replied, turning to him from her sitting position. Her eyes bulged.

In his hand was the zombie skin that she had been wearing until just minutes ago. She tensed up nervously, and Yuuhei said what she was afraid of hearing.

"Ruri, are you the serial killer Hollywood?"

His words were fairly certain, so she cast around for some kind of denial, but—

"That doctor informed me that your body is abnormal."

So…he does know.

Denying it or playing coy would not get her anywhere. Ruri looked down to avoid the iron mask of his face, and neither confirmed nor denied it.

"If that's what you thought…why didn't you hand me over to the police?"

"Did you want me to? If that's the case, I recommend turning yourself in."

"…No, that's not what I mean…"

"Then why are you upset about it?" Yuuhei said in his usual

monotone, getting to his feet. Whatever conclusion about Hollywood he took from Ruri's question, he silently reached out to take the empty water cup from her hand.

"…I see," Ruri said quietly.

Her arm instantly shot out and grabbed Yuuhei by the neck. She threw him onto the bed, ignoring the scream of all her body's muscles, and spun so that she was sitting on top of him.

With an extended finger pointed right at Yuuhei's throat, she asked, in a quiet voice thick with pressure, "Then…you couldn't have foreseen this possibility?"

"…"

Yuuhei remained expressionless. Ruri's voice grew more irritated.

"I'm going to be honest with you, Yuuhei. I know that this attitude you display is not just another act…but it's abnormal."

"Do you think so?"

"Yes. You must be crazy, letting a mass murderer into your own home."

He looked at her curiously as she sat on top of him. Ruri quietly raised her hand to strike and asked a question.

"Did you never even think it was remotely possible…that you would be killed?"

♂♀

Two hours later, Sunshine, Sixtieth Floor Street, Ikebukuro

"Good grief. This is what you get for being too good at your job. Two cases in one night!" Shinra lamented as he walked through Ikebukuro at night, the money he earned safely stashed in his doctor's briefcase. It was a line that a real doctor would rightfully punch him for saying.

"I've still got time, so maybe I should stop back in at Yuuhei's place and get those autographs," he decided, strolling through the commercial district that was markedly quieter after hours.

"Hey, is that him?"

"Yeah, it is!"

"No doubt about it!"

"Cameraman!"

"?"

Shinra noticed a sudden swell of conversation approaching and looked up to see a sudden blinding camera flash.

"Aaah!!"

"Um, excuse me! You just left an apartment owned by Yuuhei Hanejima about two hours ago, didn't you?"

"...?!"

It wasn't until the fifth camera flash that Shinra realized these men were what the world called "paparazzi."

"Do you have a moment? We understand that Yuuhei Hanejima owns all of the apartments in that building. Are you an acquaintance of his?!"

Gwuh?! No way! He's that rich?!

Shinra knew the story of how he made nearly 1.2 billion yen for his nest egg, but it was almost impossible to believe that he had enough money to buy an entire building full of the already-expensive luxury apartments that he and Celty lived in. But there was no time to dwell on that.

"About an hour ago, Hanejima and the actress Ruri Hijiribe were seen kissing out in front of the building. What do you know about their relationship?"

"What sort of medical needs were you attending to in the middle of the night?"

"What is your area of medical expertise?"

"Are you an obstetrician?!"

Reporters for a number of different sources deluged him in a waterfall of voices, voices, voices.

"H-hey! Hey, wait!"

What?! What? What happened between those two?! A kiss, just like that! What about our autographs?!

A number of suspicions arose in Shinra's panicked mind, but he could tell that the onslaught of questions and camera flashes was robbing him of his ability to think straight.

"All right... In that case, I'll be answering all of your questions after these quick messages from our sponsors...via airmail!" Shinra said and raced off in a full sprint.

"Hey, he's getting away!"

"Wait, please!"

"Just one comment!"

And as he glanced back at the pursuing reporters and cameramen over his shoulder, Shinra Kishitani experienced his first serious physical exertion in several years.

Without realizing that on the very same night, Celty was also being hounded by TV cameras.

♂♀

Twelve hours later, near Kawagoe Highway, apartment building

"Even thinking about it now, yesterday gives me the willies."

Shinra was still swaddled in black thread, wriggling around on the floor as he waited for Celty to return home.

"Honestly, I wonder what happened there... Once I get free of this, I'm going to watch the news. I was shouting about how I'd sue them for violating my likeness rights, so I doubt they used any photos of me," he muttered, a giant black silkworm flopping around on the floor seeking the TV remote before the variety shows began.

But just as he had found the remote, the doorbell rang.

Oh, damn. I can't answer the door. Wait...maybe this thread can be removed with the strength of two people?

He began to wonder what sort of story he could tell this visitor to convince them to help. But before he could call out that he was there, he heard the sound of the door unlocking.

"Oh, is that Celty?! Thank goodness! Your little abandonment fetish thing was quite exciting for a while, but I think it's finally—" he started, a look of bliss on his face as he greeted...

A number of menacing-looking men led by a gaunt-faced fellow.

It was clear from a glance that they were not in an upstanding line of work, but the thin man at the center of the group, at least, seemed like any other person in his manner.

He strode right into Shinra's home and coldly noted, "I really don't get that abandonment kink shit."

"...Oh, Mr. Shiki. What brings me the pleasure today?"

The man named Shiki looked at Shinra with a combination of

caution, relief, and amusement. The group was from the Awakusu-kai yakuza, and Shiki was a chief lieutenant in the organization despite his relative youth.

"I'm guessing you don't have a sudden patient for me," Shinra said. As a matter of fact, he had given Shiki a spare keycard for that very purpose.

A black-market doctor's most reliable and frequent clients came from their particular line of work, so Shiki's spare key allowed him to ferry patients inside in an emergency, even if Shinra was sleeping.

But none of the people present appeared to be suffering from gunshot wounds. It was rather curious.

Shiki's face got serious, and he tossed a newspaper on the ground in front of the human caterpillar. It was the day's tabloid paper with the front headline reading "Hanejima & Hijiribe's Late-Night Secret Pregnancy Date?!"

The article contained text that clearly referenced Shinra. It claimed that an obstetrician was witnessed leaving their apartment shortly before the two actors were sighted sharing a kiss.

Shinra read the article closely, relieved that at least they hadn't published a photo of his face. But...

"You do realize...that there are no other guys who wander around this neighborhood wearing white doctor's coats all the time," one of the yakuza muttered. Shiki squatted down to Shinra's eye level.

"We only have one question for you, Doctor."

"What is it?"

"Did you happen to *examine Ruri Hijiribe*?"

"Well, yes," Shinra admitted.

Shiki's face was a blank, emotionless mask, but in a different way than Yuuhei's. "I'll be direct with you—*what is she?*" he asked, his voice calm, powerful, and demanding.

Unaffected, Shinra remained light and aloof. "Before I answer that...I have a request."

His face got pale and deadly serious. He had business of the utmost importance to conduct.

"Can you help me get free of these black ropes?"

"I've been holding it in for hours, and I really need to go..."

CHAPTER 5
IKEBUKURO GUIDE BOOK
IKEBUKURO STRIKES BACK II:
TALES OF VIOLENCE IN IKEBUKURO

In the future

An excerpt from the foreword of Ikebukuro Strikes Back II

Hi.

Just to start with, I am not going to reveal my identity, and you probably wouldn't believe me, even if I did.

So let me just say that I will not reveal my own existence to you. In exchange, you are free to imagine whatever you like about me.

For one thing, I am almost entirely unrelated to any of the events I will describe in this book. I did have a small part to play in the Night of the Ripper, but it was only within the limited influence of the Internet, which is to say that I was barely involved at all.

Basically...I just watched.

That's all I did: watched.

I said that I would not reveal my identity, but I can tell you my name.

My name is Shinichi. Shinichi Tsukumoya.

But that doesn't really mean anything, so you don't need to bother remembering it.

An excerpt from Ikebukuro Strikes Back II, *Chapter 5: The Knight of Shadow Rides in the Sun.*

*   *   *

Are you aware of the motorcycle gang incident that transpired one spring afternoon in Ikebukuro this year?

A number of different gangs were fighting for territory and racing through the streets, creating traffic conditions as unsafe as a tornado or Spain's running of the bulls. For one thing, they were fighting as they rode. It must have been quite a shocking sight to the passing residents, tourists, and shoppers. It's said that a single police motorcyclist brought the incident under control. But what was the cause of it?

It was the existence of the very polar opposite of that white chopper—the Black Rider.

Shortly before the incident, the Internet was ablaze. Triggered by shocking footage (covered in another chapter) aired on live TV, a major talent agency placed a massive bounty on the man (or woman) who rode the infamous black motorcycle. A bounty worth ten million yen.

For the next several days, many people chased that dream: the ability to earn as much as the grand prize of the nation's most famous comedy contest or winning a trivia quiz game show, just for following a motorcyclist around and revealing his or her identity.

It only lasted a few days because the ensuing uproar resulted in the outrage of the police and authorities, local citizens, and other clients of the talent agency, and thus the bounty was promptly withdrawn.

This caused quite a stir. The bounty was a big story in the papers the next day and made headlines again when it was removed, and with the startling TV footage of the Black Rider turning the motorcycle into a horse, the nation was gripped with a fresh new supernatural urban legend boom.

Debate still rages about the veracity of that footage—but I know the truth.

I just won't write it down here.

As I said in the foreword, I will not interfere in the events of this city.

I needed to stick closely to a policy of observing events without taking part in order to write this book.

At any rate, I will not be disclosing the identity of the Black Rider in this book.

I do know it. But whether or not you believe me is up to you, dear readers.

*   *   *

In the same way, the Ikebukuro Motorcycle Gang Incident has its own background.

Based on the results, one might think that it was merely a number of rowdy gangsters from another prefecture that briefly invaded the city, then went back home.

But no. *Something happened.*

Something that wasn't reported in the papers or on TV.

I know what it was that happened, but I choose not to reveal it here.

If you really want to learn about it, I invite you to search for the truth on your own.

There is always more to the story.

But you cannot learn that truth without paying a price for it.

Ultimately, if you want to learn everything, you have to be involved in it and experience the truth for yourself.

It was the same for me. I just watched.

So while I know the truth that transpired behind the scenes, I don't know what the people involved were really thinking. It goes without saying that those who were directly involved know exactly how they felt about it.

That's what this means. So if you really want to find the secret truth of the matter, you have to spend something—money, time, obligation—and read the world like a book with your own hands.

If you're strong, you might also be able to wrestle the truth out of those involved, as well.

But I wouldn't recommend that. The consequences could be fatal.

Of course, if you're tough enough to beat a debt collector dressed as a bartender, then be my guest.

But that's a story for another time.

♂♀

At present, highway, Ikebukuro

"Wait, beeyotch!"

"Mohfgaa!"

"Dshbaaag!"

"Drfthjk!"

The young men on their motorcycles surrounded Celty on the road, screeching cries that didn't even qualify as language.

Oh no... How did it come to this?!

More and more bikers had flooded out of nowhere, and behind them all was a van that looked to belong to a TV news crew.

Do all of you want that ten million yen so badly?! Just do your jobs and save up fifty thousand every month for two hundred months! she thought to herself, a commonsense bit of advice that was also rather extreme.

Celty squeezed the handlebars and prepared to pump more juice into her partner. *Sorry about this, Shooter!*

The motorcycle read its owner's thoughts perfectly and let out a piercing horse bray rather than an engine roar, leaping forward as if on a spring.

"Wh-wh-whaa—?!" one of the bikers screeched. He couldn't be blamed for his shock; the bike right in front of him leaped upward six feet into the air from a flat position on the street.

The enormous shadow tilted diagonally and cleared the guardrail, proceeding over the sidewalk and the heads of the shocked onlookers. It landed on the *side* of the building, riding with its sidecar perpendicular to the ground.

To make sure that Celty's cargo—a human-sized bag with an arm hanging out of it—didn't fall out of the sidecar, a hand made out of shadow grew out of the bike and held it in place.

The bikers on the street were wide-eyed with shock at the string of unbelievable sights, but their hold on reality was so tenuous that it seemed to snap, and instead they produced a series of threats that almost seemed more indignant than threatening.

"What the hell kinda magic trick is that?!"

"You wanna get sawed in half?!"

"I'm gonna pull a rabbit outta yer ass!"

Aaaah! I knew I shouldn't have taken on this horrifying cargo!

For a moment, Celty's thoughts returned to the past.

♂♀

Thirty minutes earlier

"I'm very sorry about this. It will be a rather bothersome job," said a tall man with a cold mask covering his mouth and nose, sunglasses over his eyes, and a hat pulled low on his brow.

He was essentially fashioned entirely out of suspicious danger signals. The man pointed out the large bag at his side and said, "I want you to handle this bag for a day."

"Handle it?"

"Yes, there's a bit of a situation… I just need you to be in possession of this for a day. Once it passes this time tomorrow, you can just dump the cargo on the side of the road, anywhere you like, or you can return it to this park, where I will dispose of it. Oh, and no inquiries about the contents, please…"

It was about the fishiest job she could imagine. On top of that, Celty had just been tagged with a bounty yesterday. Worried that it might be a bomb or a transmitter of some kind, she made her suspicions quite clear with body language as she typed out, *"…I'm sorry, but who introduced you to me?"*

"An information dealer named Izaya Orihara."

"…Oh. That explains it."

I should have known.

It wasn't the first (or second) time she'd received such an eerie job offer. A couple times she had even gotten requests like, "One of my men tried to make his own bomb—schlep it out to the mountains and take care of it." The outcome of those jobs could have been inserted into any action blockbuster.

And nearly every single person whose request contained a backstory that likely involved things she didn't want to know about had come to her via Izaya Orihara.

Celty thought it over and noticed that the bag was just about big enough to fit an entire person inside. Alarms went off in her mind.

I have ferried a person on tranquilizers…but that was from Izaya himself, she recalled, shaking her head. That was about a year ago.

Normally, I would accept it, but given the circumstances...I should decline.

"I'm sorry, but I am a courier. If you need a safe, might I recommend the bank?"

"Yes, I'm aware of that. But could you make an exception?"

"*No means—*" she started typing, then stopped. The man was holding out a white envelope, looking around carefully to make sure they weren't being watched.

"Given the nature of the job, I can pay the full amount up front... I only hope the amount meets your satisfaction."

Inside the envelope, there weren't as many Yukichi Fukuzawas as she had lost the day before, but 80 percent of them was good enough. Celty erased her half-written sentence and strung together a new one in less than a second.

"I would be happy to do this for you!"

♂♀

At present, highway, Ikebukuro

I really shouldn't have taken on that job. I was too happy to make up what I lost the day before. I got carried away.

But it was too late for regret.

The motorcycle officer had already seen the arm dangling out of the bag. Up until then, she'd only been guilty of traffic infractions, which were simply ticketed on sight. But if she became suspected of murder or dumping a body, they would set up a proper investigation. The thought plunged Celty into despair.

I can handle being chased by the police. But I can't take the idea of not living with Shinra anymore!

What was the statute of limitations on disposing of a dead body? Could she be charged with it if no body was ever found?

Celty leaped off the side of the building and landed on the face of another one. It was the kind of eerie sight one saw only in CG, but the easy skill of the motion only made the whole thing less real to those who saw it.

Shit, I took the job knowing this might happen...and I knew that I wasn't doing a job that was conducive to a stable life...but I still can't afford to get caught now! At least let me just leave Ikebukuro so those I care about aren't affected...

She was thinking as if she were caught already. In her resignation, the faces of those she knew flashed through her head, like her life passing before her eyes before death.

So much happened in the last year... I met Mikado and joined the Dollars... I got to be friends with Anri...and most importantly, Shinra and I...

...

Shinra...

No! Enough of that!

She was swallowed with both love and grief, but it wasn't the time for emotional reflection.

Keep it together, Celty! Just do...something! Make sure things work out, and things'll work out!

"God helps those who help themselves," the saying went, but Celty wasn't going to rest on her laurels and hope for the best. She focused forward and headed down a side street, hoping to escape her pursuers.

Riding on the side of a building meant she had no reason to fear a collision with oncoming or merging traffic. She spread her shadow over the surface of the structure and shifted directions without a noticeable loss of speed, splitting apart the bikers chasing her.

But she knew it was only a temporary fix. She turned down another street, hoping to return to the main road and put some real distance between them, when a familiar van passed right by her, driving on the road like a vehicle should.

Wasn't that...?

It was a box van with an unforgettable feature on the side door—a gaudy painting of an anime character.

Kadota, Yumasaki, and Karisawa's van!

The fact that it was actually Togusa's would be cold comfort to him. Meanwhile, Celty slowed down—and noticed that something was wrong.

Huh? Wait a minute. What happened?!

The van was dented all over, and the windows were cracked, as though they'd just driven through a minor riot. Celty pulled off the surface of the building wall and sidled up next to the van.

All of a sudden, a storm of voices erupted from the vehicle.

"...Black Rider!"

"Celty?!"

"...Celty!"

"Oh, Celcchi."

"Hey, that's Celty."

"What's this? What's going on, Mr. Ryuugamine?!"

"Ohh! It's the Black Rider! Look, Kuru, the Black Rider!"

"...No way."

Inside the van, Celty saw several familiar and unfamiliar faces alike, to her surprise. She pulled up and matched the speed of the car, subtly hiding the contents of the sidecar in shadow as she used one hand to steer and the other to type.

"Sorry, I'm being chased by a motorcycle gang! Run for it!"

"..."

Kadota looked at her desperate message and smirked. "Sorry, but... we might be the ones who need to apologize, Black Rider."

Huh?

An obnoxious car horn went off behind them. Celty turned around and saw, sure enough, a group of bikers.

"We're being chased, too."

The fresh mass of violence and anger joined up with the gang pursuing Celty, forming a fleet of over fifty vehicles that bore down on them with the force of a typhoon and the human rage of a mob.

"Is it hopeless?"

"Nah, we got one bit of hope on our side."

Celty's helmet tilted questioningly, prompting Kadota to grin wickedly.

"They're all *outsiders*, while we're part of the Dollars, right?"

"When people come and raise hell in your territory...it gives you the justification to fight back."

♂♀

Two hours in the past, Ikebukuro

"Hey, you guys," Kadota said. The young men surrounding the two girls turned to him with disgust.

"Whaa—? Hell are you?"

"Hell you want? Uhh?" they growled at him menacingly. Kadota twisted and popped his neck vertebrae.

"Thought it was kinda funny that you needed four grown men to pick a fight with two little girls."

"..."

"Lemme see your stickers. I'll write a new name on 'em. I'm thinking 'the Pedo Gang' has a nice ring to it."

"Shuddup! Buzz off and die!" they retorted. One of the thugs reached out and grabbed Kadota by the shirt. The next moment, Kadota took advantage of the momentum to slam his forehead right into the man's nose.

"*Guh?!* Dah...bwlah!"

The thug fell backward, sputtering with rage as blood shot out of his broken nose a second later.

"Damn. That ain't cool, face-butting a guy's forehead. What if I have a skull fracture?" Kadota grumbled, rubbing his forehead as he stood over the fallen thug, who was clutching his head in both hands.

The leering smiles of the other three thugs vanished at Kadota's shameless insistence that he was the real victim, replaced by glares of rage and caution.

"You bi...aaaaaaauugahaaaaaa! —! —! —!"

"?!"

A thug started screaming suddenly, drawing the attention of everyone else present.

One of them was writhing with his hands over his crotch, while the girl in the gym clothes clutched her bag tight in both hands.

One look at the man cradling his genitals with his eyes rolled back was enough to tell the entire story. And as everyone was taken aback by the sight, the other girl with the reserved glasses leaped off a nearby motorcycle to deliver a kick straight to the jaw of the man standing next to her, unconcerned with the billowing of her skirt.

She was wearing safety shoes with metal plates in the toes. Ironically, this made the shoe very unsafe to the target of her kick.

"Fbweh..."

The man wobbled, then lost the support of his legs and fell to the ground.

There was only one left. Karisawa and Yumasaki were already tying up the man with the bloody nose, binding his wrists together with the headband cloth he had been wearing.

The unhurt thug glanced at the two girls for an angry second but settled on delivering his final line to Kadota instead.

"...Y-you...fuckers... You'll pay for this! You in the bandanna!"

Apparently, he was deciding to blame it all on Kadota, so as to avoid admitting that teenage girls had anything to do with it.

As Kadota watched him ride off, he turned back and noted, "We don't want him calling the cops, and it's bad news if he calls his friends, too, so we oughta scram," to the girls dressed in uniform and gym clothes.

"Huh? And you are...?"

"Kadota. You're Izaya's sisters, right?"

"What?! You know Iza?! Oh...actually, I might have met you before!" Mairu exclaimed in surprise. Kururi bowed deeply to Kadota, apparently realizing from the very start that these were acquaintances of her brother.

"...Thank you...very much."

"Nah, it's cool. Maybe you didn't need our help after all...but you do stick out, so if you're going somewhere, we can call our car around. What do you say?"

"Wow, really?!"

"Just don't expect any rides to Hokkaido or anything," Kadota cautioned wryly.

Mairu waved her hands in excitement. "Oh, um, oh! We're just wandering all over Ikebukuro today! We're supposed to get a call from someone we know, but we won't know *when and where to go* until the call arrives!"

"...What's that supposed to mean...? Whatever. The other two back there are supposed to be guiding some students from your school around Ikebukuro, so I guess you could just tag along with them. Okay?" he asked, turning back to Karisawa and Yumasaki. They thought it over for a few seconds.

"Umm, I don't see a problem."

"Not an issue. Besides, those girls look kinda 2-D to me, anyway."

"Shut up."

And so, despite the very tenuous relationship that connected them, the two groups wound up moving around together. Kadota recommended several times that the girls return home, but they were insistent on their task, and he didn't pry any further.

Well, if it comes down to it, I can call Izaya and tell him to take them, Kadota told himself and called up Togusa. He took the group to a nearby café so they could wait for the van to arrive.

And a while later, when they were ready to pile into Togusa's van, a gang of motorcycle thugs five times the size of the earlier group descended upon them, kicking off a mad rush for safety.

♂♀

At present, inside Togusa's van, highway, Ikebukuro

"So that one thug pretended to run away, but secretly he was following us. That way, his gang was ready to jump us when we left the café."

"It's like they were raised entirely on manga about delinquents and street gangs."

"No way, Karisawa! Delinquent mangas always feature a truly manly protagonist who protects the weak and fights the strong! If they were using that stuff as a textbook, they wouldn't have been harassing girls in the first place!"

"Maybe they were so dumb that they didn't understand the lesson the textbook was teaching?"

"...Ohhh! No wonder!"

Karisawa and Yumasaki's chatter was basically the same as it ever was, despite the imminent danger of dozens of pursuing motorcycles.

"Wh-what should we do about this? Call the cops?" Mikado asked, but Kadota shook his head.

"They've gotta know about this by now! And I saw that one guy on the police bike earlier! The question is just if we can stay away from them until the police are finally on the scene in full force. I might be able to handle them ganging up on us with metal pipes, but not you kids."

"G-good point..."

"Don't worry, we're gonna make sure that you students get away, at the very least. I'll drive you right into police headquarters if I have to," Kadota growled from the passenger seat. Mikado started to exhale with relief, then chastised himself.

No! We need to help Sonohara, Aoba, and those two girls escape to safety...but I can't just run with them and leave the other Dollars and Celty behind in danger!

He gritted his teeth against the fear creeping into him and remembered when he charged into the Yellow Scarves' hideout and when he first met Celty.

I might die...but...I have to do something...

Mikado clenched his fists. Aoba looked over and hesitantly asked, "Mr. Ryuugamine, are you okay?"

"Huh? O-oh, I'm fine. Sorry, you'll have to make do on your own..."

"No, I mean... You know what, never mind."

"?"

Mikado wondered what Aoba was trying to say. But then he looked out the window.

There was a black sidecar of sorts affixed to Celty's motorcycle with some kind of cargo stashed inside of it.

"I guess...since Celty's under a bounty now..."

He paused. It was just an instant of a pause, and then he said something that didn't seem very appropriate, given their circumstances.

"I suppose...we won't be able to just see her hanging around anymore..."

♂♀

The Black Rider kept pace alongside Togusa's van as the bikers chased behind them.

Everyone inside the van was also being chased, including some who weren't originally involved: Celty, Kadota, Togusa, Karisawa, Yumasaki, Mikado, Anri, Aoba, Kururi, and Mairu.

A total of ten people on the run.

If it were only the motorcycle gang, Celty could handle them on her own. The problem was that staying still to deal with them would only give the motor officers time to surround her.

But wait. If I do that, at least it would ensure that everyone inside the van is taken to safety, she thought, looking behind her. There were more pursuers now, and two helicopters that probably belonged to the TV station, hovering overhead.

Damn! I can't let them all be known associates of a dead-body dumper... At worst, they'll all be identified on live TV!

Kadota's group was one thing, but if Anri, Mikado, and the other students were identified in connection to this horrible incident, the consequences would be terrible. If they were exposed as having connections to Celty—or the other gang squabbles prior to this—they could easily be expelled from school.

What do I do? What should I do, what should I do?!

Until now, she had been alone.

It was years ago that she started working as a courier here, but she'd never been racked by a problem like this before. Back then, everyone else, including Shinra, was just a stranger to her.

Even facing the risk of being captured, killed, or exposed to the rest of the world posed a limited risk—it was her problem, no one else's. So she set about doing her job.

But now, it was different. After the incident a year ago, she and Shinra were no longer strangers.

She'd met many other people, and in just the span of a year, the world around her changed dramatically.

She wasn't alone anymore. And it was only now that she understood the shackles of that truth.

...

All she could think about was the many idle conversations she shared with Shinra at home.

♂♀

Several weeks earlier, Shinra's apartment

"The fairy from a foreign land living in Ikebukuro, Celty! The headless dullahan plunged into Ikebukuro in search of her missing head and memories! But when she fell in love with a man named Shinra, the search for her head became nothing but an excuse for her new life sinking ever deeper into love!"

*   *   *

"…Which, if you think about it, shows that Celty isn't exactly a *tsundere*! She's an all new type of character, somewhere between the *tsundere* and the straight-up cool type!"

"Come on, Yumacchi. Your definition of *tsundere* is way too strict. Just accept that she's a *tsundere*."

"Celty's not like that, I'm telling you. If anything, she's too efficient at her job… She's straightforward, but not entirely coolheaded. More like an old-fashioned, empathetic older-sister type! The older sister who relies upon an unreliable older brother… That's it! She's an older younger sister!"

"That is way too complicated."

Yumasaki and Karisawa babbled on in debate as they stuck their legs under the heated blanket of the kotatsu that served as a low table. At the nearby dining table, a different man and woman exchanged a much colder topic.

"Hey, Shinra."

"What is it, Celty? You look serious."

"Why have they come into our home, and why are they talking about me at length? On that note…how did they learn my personal information?"

"Well, I might as well come clean, since you'll find out sooner or later. I ran into Kadota's group at a bar earlier…and these two were carrying on and on about your incredible rumors, so…"

"…"

"So I bragged that you were my girlfriend… And I'll say this, too, since I'm sure you'll find out—I also included some rather salacious info about this, that, and the other thing that you did on our dates… I tell you, the power of alcohol is terrifying. Ouch, ouch, ouch! What was that for, Celty?! You see, I knew you were a *tsundere*-ow-ow-ow-ow-ow-ow!"

"If that's what you want, I'll do what a tsundere does. Before I get all lovey-dovey on you, I have to be a bit more pokey-pokey with my shadow."

"If that's what you call poking, I'd say it's more like stabby-stabby, but—aaaaaiieeee!!"

*   *   *

As they continued on in their usual way, Yumasaki and Karisawa took note in *their* usual way.

"See? She's a *tsundere*."

"I disagree. They're too straightforward about their shared love for her to be a *tsundere*. It's more like a soft S-and-M relationship, where Celty gets mentally punished, while Kishitani gets physically punished... And neither of them seems to be enjoying it, so they're both on the sadist side!"

"That is way too complicated."

♂♀

Celty shook with chuckling laughter as she recalled that silly moment in time.

"My girlfriend," he called me. The truth is…that made me really happy.

I got too carried away over the past year. I was too happy.

She mentally chided herself on her own softness. And once she was done feeling irritation at herself…

She thought.

She cared.

But still…

Celty fashioned a third arm out of shadow that typed away at her PDA for her as she rode.

I mean, still…

As she paced the van, she tossed the device through the open window to Kadota in the passenger seat.

That doesn't mean I can just give up on it.

"…! Hey, Black Rider…you serious about this?" Kadota asked as he returned her PDA. She held a thumb up.

"…All right. Listen, Black Rider. I know what your name is, but since I didn't hear it from you, it didn't feel right to say it myself. So this'll be weird, but…"

Celty had never had a proper conversation with this man before. He looked back at her, deadly serious, and gave her a thumbs-up of his own.

"Let me thank you afterward, Celty."

*   *   *

And with that, Celty made up her mind, the silent determination calming her heart.

That's right. No matter who, no matter what, no matter when, I don't give up on my connections.

I can't give them up.

Without my head, what else do I have left?

And with force of will, Celty silently produced a giant scythe out of her hand. Waving it back and forth to keep the pursuers behind them at bay, she joined Kadota's van in heading for the same location.

They stayed fairly close, and they were lucky enough not to get stuck with a light. As a matter of fact, the biker gangs were raising hell here and there, causing the normal traffic to stop for safety.

Thanks to this bit of good luck, Celty and the van were able to reach their destination in just a minute or so: the tunnel that passed under the railway, connecting the east and west gates of the Ikebukuro Station.

The van continued straight through the tunnel. But Celty spun her partner around, bringing the Coiste Bodhar to a sudden stop with a horrific screech that was not at all like tires squealing.

Dozens of motorcycles bore down on her.

Ironically, the hint came from the motorcycle cop.

As well as her conversation with Shinra that morning.

Celty timed the moment and held her enormous scythe aloft.

In the next moment, like a giant spiderweb, countless tiny ropes extended from the scythe to catch everywhere along the tunnel and form an enormous net.

♂♀

At that moment, Medei-gumi Syndicate, Awakusu-kai Office

The Awakusu-kai was one of the offices of the Medei-gumi crime syndicate, one of several organizations that claimed territory within Ikebukuro.

The room in the back of the office contained all of the things you would expect to see, based on the televised yakuza dramas: the luxurious wooden desk, the picture frames, the black leather couch. But the entrance looked like any other business office.

It was perfectly "office-like," but one would be hard-pressed to identify what kind of business they actually ran at a glance. And it was this place where Kazamoto, one of the group's officers, listened quietly to a status report.

"...So it seems like there's some biker gangs from out of town raising hell in the streets..."

"As long as they're not interfering with our affiliated businesses, leave them be. The government employees will use our hard-earned taxes to handle this."

The young lieutenant had sharp, reptilian eyes. He followed up his sardonic comment by asking the subordinate, "What's happening with the Yodogiri situation?"

"Well, Mr. Shiki's gone to the usual doctor."

Kazamoto steepled his fingers on his cheeks and tapped away at his face. "The thing is, I don't really care. I don't care about the Headless Rider, monsters, ghosts, aliens, any of that occult shit. It's fine if it's real, fine if it ain't."

"Y-yes, sir."

"The problem is...we were hired to *take care* of a young female star...and now she's gone and messed up four of our men. Normally, I'd punish them for being soft, then do whatever it takes to eliminate the target, but..."

The lizard-like man paused. His subordinate nervously prompted, "B-but this is different?"

"Yes... Our client had the gall to hide something from us and, as a result, exposed our people to danger. Ordinarily, this means holding the client who disrespected us responsible for that outcome," he said icily.

The other man tried to ignore the cold sweat breaking out on his skin as he replied, "R-right, sir. But...I heard we didn't have plans to kill the girl or anything..."

For a moment, Kazamoto took his gaze off the subordinate, and the temperature of his voice rose slightly. "I hate to mention this, but...

while it's true that the client asked for her to be buried in the mountains, we were actually planning to just ship her off overseas or to one of our 'special partners' out in the boonies."

"Y-yes, sir. But why would—?"

"This is absolutely classified information," Kazamoto said, fixing his man in place with his sharpest gaze yet. He then spun around in his chair to deliver the uncomfortable, awkward truth.

"The target, Ruri Hijiribe, reminds the boss of his daughter—the one who went off and got married to a civilian. He's a big fan of the girl... and so are several of the muckety-mucks up in the Medei-gumi..."

"I...see...," the subordinate replied awkwardly.

Not wanting to leave his bosses the only source of embarrassment, Kazamoto quietly admitted, "And so am I...and Shiki... I mean, she's just really abnormally hot, you know."

♂♀

The previous night, Yuuhei Hanejima's apartment

"Did you never even think it was remotely possible...that you would be killed?"

A man pressed down on a bed.

A killer on top straddling him.

Easily pierced through the heart with the slice of a hand, the news reported.

It was an absolutely deadly and helpless situation for him—but the young man didn't make a sound.

In fact, it was the killer's raised hand that was trembling uncertainly.

In just a few seconds, the Hollywood killer, Ruri Hijiribe, felt like several minutes had passed.

Her wits spaced out several times. Her vision warped, as she battled the momentary sense that she was not herself anymore.

By the time her lips started trembling, Ruri could no longer bear the silence. So it was the utmost salvation when the man below her finally opened his mouth to speak.

"...Can I ask one thing?"

"...What?"

"If you killed me right now, would it be to silence me?"

"...I suppose it would," Ruri said, averting her eyes as she listened to Yuuhei Hanejima's flat voice.

No, this is all wrong. I wouldn't kill someone to silence them...

Her body vibrated violently, and Ruri realized that it was fear she was experiencing.

Nausea and chills stole over her. Even her heart seemed to be going solid in her chest.

Besides, I can't kill him. Whether through calculation or instinct, I don't think I can kill this man.

And not just this man. I don't think I can kill anyone aside from them.

What did her face look like at that moment?

From his position below her, Yuuhei said, his voice still quiet and expressionless, "Then, I think you probably shouldn't do it."

"...?"

It was an odd thing for Yuuhei to say. She squinted down at him questioningly. His eyes were endlessly cold and dry, completely hiding the true emotions that lingered behind the mask.

"The security cameras have footage of me bringing you in here. You're in the footage, too, of course."

"...!"

"The camera footage is saved somewhere, but you don't know where, do you? So killing me to keep me from talking won't really do you any good," he said calmly.

Ruri muscled her chills into submission and asked, "What if I just feel like killing you?"

"Then, I can't help that. I'd rather not be killed, though," he said simply.

He was certainly more than a little successful in his life, but Ruri still felt like something was off in his confession.

"I'm surprised to hear that. You'd rather not be killed?"

"Not really. I would have a little regret left if I died here."

"..."

Her eyes went wide. She felt like she was watching some odd, eccentric creature dance and couldn't help but chuckle. The shivers and nausea didn't stop, but she couldn't keep herself from chuckling at him, herself, and everything.

"What's so funny?"

"Ha-ha... Oh, it's just...so strange to hear a total robot like you talk about 'regrets'... What in the world could a mannequin like you care about to regret losing it?"

"Well, there's some movie stuff I haven't finished filming yet..."

He paused, his face blank, as he searched for the right words.

Eventually, he found them.

"I suppose the biggest regret would be having a girl about to cry right in front of me and being unable to help."

As soon as he said those words, devoid of any kind of facial or vocal emotion, time stopped between them.

"..."

"..."

There was nothing in Yuuhei's eyes. But that also meant there was no hint of a joke or self-aggrandizing pretension, either.

After a long silence, Ruri spoke, her hand still raised in the chopping position.

"Are you hitting on me...? Or are you just desperate to survive and trying to get on my good side?"

"Good question. Even I don't really know. People say that I don't understand others, and they say they don't understand what I'm thinking. I agree. I don't understand myself. But I do know some things."

"..."

"Like a man who watches a girl asking for help and doesn't try to stop her tears is the worst."

The young man's face was so blank and cool that he transcended being a robot and reached the realm of some kind of transcendental being. Ruri began to wonder if he was just a hallucination. She was barely able to wrench out the words, "That's a line...from *Carmilla Saizou*..."

"Yes, he's one of the figures I respect most."

"Respect? A character that you play...?" she asked in exasperation, thinking of the movie that they had once worked on together.

But that accusation didn't faze Yuuhei in the least. "That's right. I've played an insane killer, an idiotic criminal, a gay man in love—and I respect each and every character I've acted."

"..."

"My brother was overemotional, so I used him as a negative role model, and now I think I'm missing a number of important things for a person to have. And I understand that—which is why I think I became an actor."

"Uh..."

"Each and every person I play in a movie gives me a little piece of their humanity," Yuuhei said with little emotion but even less shame. Even facing death like this, he did not beg for mercy but laid his heart bare. Ruri couldn't help but lower her hand.

He's the opposite. The very opposite of me.

I'm a human trying to be a monster. But he's a monster.

A monster who wants to be human.

He didn't possess terrible strength. He didn't blow fire, and he wasn't immortal.

And yet, Ruri could sense that the man before her was mentally *alien*.

It was at this point that she realized her eyes were leaking tears. But whether they were tears of sadness or some other emotion was beyond her.

Which must be what makes him...so much more human than me.

This man wanted everything that she was trying to discard. What should she think about him?

Pity? Empathy? Disgust? Or just label him a resident of another world and ignore him?

She didn't even have the answer to that question now.

It was all confusion.

All the emotions she'd been trying to get rid of swirled and churned, washing away her monstrous mask.

"...I'm sorry. I never thanked you for saving me," Ruri mumbled, getting off of Yuuhei and sitting next to the bed. "Thank you. You... saved my life."

"You don't have to thank me."

"Why…? In fact…why did you save me to begin with?"

"Well, I mean…I did it whether you were Hollywood or not."

That's when Ruri realized that, for just one instant, Yuuhei's face contained a hint of trouble.

"I was wondering what kind of person could do this to someone as nimble and powerful as you…and…I came up with one possibility."

"?"

"Does this have anything to do with…a man in a bartender outfit and sunglasses?"

Ruri looked up in shock at her savior's question. In her mind, she saw the true monster, who had slammed her into the sky with a bench.

"Do you…know him?

"…I had a feeling it was him…" Yuuhei sighed, then quietly got to his feet. "I can tell you more about him in the future. I need to apologize to you."

"Apologize?"

She gaped at him in total bewilderment, but Ruri did not receive an explanation on the spot. The actor turned toward the computer monitor in the room and said, "By the way, there's one thing I'd like to retroactively confirm."

"…What is it?" she asked. She wasn't sure whether to be polite or open and frank with him. She decided that it would be best just to avoid displeasing him.

"As a matter of fact, while you were passed out, it seems like we were followed. According to Kishita…the doctor earlier, they didn't seem to belong to proper civilian professions."

"Uh…"

"So I took it upon myself to get some insurance."

♂♀

Entrance, Yuuhei Hanejima's apartment building

"Hey, there she is."

"There's a man with her. What's the plan?"

"Just knock 'em out."

"And do it quietly… Let's move."

Four men dressed in handyman uniforms peered out of a shady alley. They snuck through the darkness without a sound, carefully approaching their targets. Once they had flanked the pair and were ready to knock them over from behind, certain of their victory—the raucous flashing and clicking of cameras stopped them in their tracks.

"?!"

The four men squinted, blinded by the sudden light. They eventually saw well over a dozen cameramen and reporters filling the street. And right in front of them, the man and woman were now embracing.

No way… Wh-when did they get here?!

Hey, they just got us in the picture!

The men had been very careful. But so had the cameramen who were waiting to get the perfect scoop.

Ruri looked down shyly as the storm of lightning flashes continued, while Yuuhei turned to a nearby reporter and asked in monotone, "How did you know?"

As if on cue, all the reporters raced forward to ask questions. They had to know that Yuuhei was the only person who ever came in or out of this building. The raucous deluge of questions and camera flashes continued despite the very late hour.

"We just had an anonymous tip!"

"What's the deal?!"

"How long have you been a couple?"

"Where did you two meet?"

"Any plans for a press conference?"

"Does your agency know?"

"When's the wedding?"

"We noticed a man wearing a white lab coat leaving earlier."

"Is he involved in this?"

"Damn, missed him!"

"Find him!"

"Call another team to go look for a guy in white!"

The four men who were supposed to abduct Ruri went completely pale. With this many people, there was no way they could retrieve the film that showed them. Not to mention that an abduction was out of the question now.

As the men gritted their teeth in frustration, Yuuhei calmly answered, "I'm sorry, but it's very late, so I will have to explain another day. We're going to go for a nice relaxing drive together now."

After a few more comments of explanation, Yuuhei took Ruri back into the building with a hand around her shoulder. A few minutes later, a car emerged and sped off.

A few reporters tried to follow them, but most of the reporting vehicles were already being used to cover the Black Rider incident, following Daioh TV's lead.

And so, in full sight of the reporters and would-be kidnappers, the star actor and serial killer disappeared into the night.

♂♀

At present, tunnel, Ikebukuro

Celty had fashioned a shadow version of an actual kind of net that was used to subdue motorcycle gangs in real life. It was meant to gently tangle and stop the bikes, ending their rampage.

Setting up such nets was rather difficult, as the timing of deployment and the possibility of the gangs scouting out the locations in advance were both exploitable weaknesses. But Celty's shadow had no such weaknesses and admirably trapped the riders.

"*Gaah!* What the hell is this?!"

"Daaagh!"

The bikers plunged one after the other into the net of shadow. As the rear vehicles saw what was happening, they slowed and stopped, leaving a huge logjam of motorcycles at one end of the tunnel and splitting it into safe and unsafe halves.

She could freely go and escape now, but that would not solve anything. Celty considered whether she should truly plant the seed of terror in them or allow them to capture her and get their ten million yen.

At the very least, the top priority of allowing Kadota's van to go free was a success. Now that the van had escaped around the west side of Ikebukuro Station, Celty decided she would surrender herself to fate.

That was the moment that Ikebukuro decided to truly get the most out of its holiday.

♂♀

At that moment, inside the van

"All right…you guys get out and either race through the station or pile into the police building nearby… As long as you tell them you just got wrapped up in this through no fault of your own, you should be fine!" Kadota said to the rest of the group once the tunnel was no longer in the rearview mirror.

He threw open the side door so the passengers could get out. Mikado tried to stay in but was forcibly pushed out by those behind him.

"What about you, Dotachin?" Karisawa asked.

Kadota looked away, then sighed. "You know Celty? She's with Shinra, right?"

"Uhh, yeah. She's such a *tsundere* with him. It makes me embarrassed to watch them."

"No, Karisawa! I keep telling you, she's an 'older younger sister'!"

Kadota ignored the two bickerers and quietly turned to Togusa in the driver's seat.

"Damn. I barely had anything to do with him in high school…so I don't really know what Shinra's like in person…but I gotta admit, I'm kinda jealous," he said, then smiled happily and continued, "Celty… she's a babe. Yeah, she's a good woman. Right, Togusa?"

"Huh? The Black Rider's a chick?"

"…Anyway, that settles it. Can't go having a girl save my ass. You know?"

Togusa seemed to understand what he meant and put his hand to the stick, wryly observing, "So, we're gonna find and retrieve the Black Rider, then escape? Or help her out?"

Kadota grinned wickedly, and Togusa gunned the engine.

♂♀

In the tunnel

So, what now?

On the other side of Celty's shadow net, a small riot was unfolding.

A number of the bikers were attempting to rip the shadow, and due to the fact that multiple rival gangs were involved, some of them appeared to be starting a fistfight.

"Dammit! I thought we had more guys than this! Get everyone in here for backup!"

"We can't! Out in front of the station…some monster cop is wipin' everybody out!"

"Shit! What's happening here?! Have you called the chief…?"

"I can't reach him! Maybe he's mad that we jumped off on our own without permission…"

"Gaah! We gotta at least kill that Black Rider and get some damn money outta this!"

What?! That bounty wasn't "dead or alive," was it?!

At this point, there was no room for negotiation. Celty turned back, prepared to flee—but then she saw a different biker gang group coming up from the other direction. It had to be the remnants of the various gangs alerted remotely.

More and more bikes began to approach, the lucky ones who had escaped the motorcycle cops.

Damn… If I put up another net on the other side of the tunnel and lock myself in…then once the bikers are gone, I'll be surrounded by the police! There'll be no way to explain away the cargo I'm carrying!

Then, from behind the oncoming swarm of bikes came a single van.

Is that them?! I told them to run for it!

Most likely the middle schoolers had been let loose, but Celty wanted Kadota and the other adults to find safety as well. She paused for a brief second, unsure of what to do…

Then saw that some of the bikers were starting to work their way through the net on their own and turned back to the original direction.

Celty fashioned a dull black scythe and tried to use it to fight them off—but something struck her as wrong.

Right to the side of her bike stood an unfamiliar shadow.

As she slowly, fearfully turned toward it, she saw a man like a mummy, his face wrapped in thick bandages.

He was standing in her sidecar. His feet were inside the now-empty black bag she was ferrying.

The man who had been her cargo spoke.

"...Leave this to me... You should escape."

♂♀

Half a day earlier, inside Russia Sushi

"...Hell of an injured patient you brought to me, damn you."

Inside a sushi bar run by two Russians, which was quickly becoming a familiar sight to Ikebukuro residents, the after-hours interior stank for reasons other than fish.

A sheet was placed over the tatami booth in the back, so that a doctor in a white coat—Shinra Kishitani—could tend to a man whose face had been shattered.

"My visit will cost you two hundred thousand yen."

"Cut me a deal."

"Can't do that. I lost the golden opportunity to spend time with Ruri Hijiribe on account of this patient."

"What the hell does that mean?"

Simon butted into the argument between the white owner and Shinra. "Oh, no good, you two fight. First, you make Egor's boo-boo say bye-bye. Please to do it, passing marks one hundred percent!"

"Fine, fine. Just make sure you arrange the money... May I assume that Egor is the patient's name?"

"That's right. We were in the same organization back in Russia, but... Oh, what the hell am I telling you for?"

As this conversation continued in the back, Mairu Orihara sat at the front counter with her sister, placing a call on her cell phone.

"...Oh! He picked up! Hello, Iza? Listen, I have a question for you!

Hey, do you recognize the name Celty Sturluson?" she excitedly asked, reading the name off of the thick envelope. But she didn't get the answer she wanted.

"…Huh? What do you mean, none of our business? So you *do* know something about this person, Iza! I knew it! Holy crap! No fair, no fair! No! Fair! Huh…?"

Mairu looked down at her phone in disbelief and began to stomp on the floor in frustration.

"…What happened?"

"I can't believe it! Iza just hung up on me! Um, well…I guess I have no choice… Here goes…"

She quietly sulked down at her phone, looked up a different contact from the last one, and grinned to herself as she hit the send button.

♂♀

At present, outside Ikebukuro Station

"Aww, man, where did Mr. Ryuugamine and Ms. Sonohara go?"

Immediately after they were let out of the van, Mikado had said, "Take care of Sonohara and the girls," and raced off. The next thing Aoba knew, Anri had also vanished.

"…I guess Mr. Ryuugamine really is…oh, never mind," Aoba muttered as he looked around. Meanwhile, Mairu and Kururi stood holding hands.

"…What should…we do?"

"Hmm, I guess we can just watch for now? I don't know what will happen, but I sure didn't expect to see her up so close!"

"…"

Kururi looked down the street that headed to the tunnel with a serious look in her eyes. Meanwhile, Mairu cackled to herself. Amid the cool breeziness of her laugh was a note of poisonous malice.

"So…I wonder if we'll be able to *introduce ourselves to Celty* properly."

♂♀

Half a day earlier, inside Russia Sushi

"Nngh..."

The man in the tatami booth opened his eyes and stared vaguely at his surroundings.

"Oh, he's awake."

The man glanced at the first figure to enter his view and, through the fog in his head, said the name, "Shingen?"

"Huh?"

Shinra was momentarily taken aback by his father's name. He examined the man's face—not that he could see much, covered in bandages as it was.

"...Oh, pardon me. I seem to have confused you for someone else..."

"..."

Shinra leaned over the prone man, thinking hard for several seconds. Eventually, he bolted upright, took out his phone, and walked toward the seats at the front counter. Two girls trotted over to take his place and stepped into the tatami booth.

"...Are you...all right?"

"Yoo-hoo! Feeling better? Good for you, buddy! It's all okay! Reconstructive surgery can work miracles these days! You even look cool in those bandages, if you don't mind me saying so!"

"Ahh... I have not thanked you two yet. Thank you for saving me."

Egor's eyes were sharp as they gazed through the bandages, but he maintained a gentlemanly demeanor. Relieved that their acquaintance would recover, Simon and the manager kicked up a conversation in Russian with Egor.

"XXXX" "XX"

"XXXXX" "XX!"

As the conversation went on, the manager's face grew more and more gloomy.

"What's up?" Mairu asked.

The manager responded, "Well...it sounds like he doesn't have a coin to his name."

"...Forgive me. I just failed the job I was pursuing... Now I wish that I had gotten some money up front."

"So what's your plan? If we just hand over two hundred thousand yen now, we can't stock the fish for tomorrow... I suppose we could just close the restaurant tomorrow, but then..."

"Oh, close store, very good. Tomorrow we celebrate Sushi Extermination Day, eat ramen, eat mochi."

"Get outta here with that bullshit," the manager grumbled. Meanwhile, Mairu squatted down on the tatami in the booth.

"Hey, you." She pulled on Egor's sleeve. He looked puzzled.

"...What?" he asked suspiciously. Mairu gave him an angelic smile.

"Shall we front you the money?"

♂♀

At present, tunnel, Ikebukuro Station

Celty was in a panic.

The cargo she was ferrying suddenly woke up and began neutralizing the oncoming bikers with his bare hands.

Even the term *smooth* failed to describe his movements. He was smoke in human form, riding the breeze and flowing between the attacking men.

When they passed by one another, his target would already be fallen. It was as though he were teaching dozens of monkeys how to dance.

Totally unsure of what was real anymore, Celty turned back toward the van. She was concerned about the safety of Kadota's team—but she found a fresh concern when she did so.

Halfway down the slope leading to the tunnel was a figure sprinting toward them at full speed.

Mikado?!

She tried to send body and hand signals to the boy to warn him to turn back, but not only did she have bigger fish to fry, it would be counterproductive if the enemy noticed Mikado because of her signals.

And behind him, on the other side of the road, she saw a busty girl with glasses.

Anri!

She knew Anri was powerful. If she used the power of the cursed blade Saika to its full extent, the girl could be even more dangerous than Celty.

But that's exactly what you shouldn't do!

Anri was keeping the fact that she was Saika a secret from everyone. If she utilized that power right here in the open—possibly with TV cameras pointed at her—it would ruin everything for her.

This was already a bewildering and frightening turn of events for Celty.

Then, Ikebukuro's holiday made it worse.

A fierce impact echoed through the tunnel, drawing the attention of everyone present. It happened on the other side of Celty's net, where the motorcycle gang members were trying to break through with dozens of bikes left behind.

The source of the sound was a motorcycle, flying as though it had been struck by a large car. And waving around a motorcycle engine in one hand—

A knight in medieval armor, *with no head.*

Huh?
Confusion reigned.
Confusion reigned.
Another one...of me...?
At first, Celty thought that perhaps another of her kind had just appeared in Ikebukuro. She did remember that back in Ireland, she sensed the presence of a number of other dullahans lurking somewhere out there.

But why here and now?

A fresh wave of doubt and confusion rolled over her—but paradoxically, the increasingly confusing images only cooled her head down.

No, this presence...doesn't belong to "us"...

But...there's something among all the humans...

It was at that point that Celty quietly recalled when she had felt that presence.

Just a few hours ago, when she'd run a job during the morning.

This aura...

It's who I transported this morning!

♂♀

Several hours earlier, warehouse, Ikebukuro

There was a warehouse sector quite a ways removed from the metropolitan center of Ikebukuro. One of the buildings, which was currently empty, served as the meeting place of Celty and her client.

The client was a stranger to her and had been introduced through Shizuo Heiwajima.

It's quite rare for Shizuo to send someone my way.

The client was a woman hiding her face with a muffler, hat, and sunglasses, and the job required Celty to take her to the designated location.

Although she did not provide a more detailed reason, the woman was apparently wanted by the mob, and it was possible that they would have a makeshift checkpoint set up along the way to detain her.

At first Celty wasn't so sure about her, but once she picked up the woman's "presence," she couldn't help but ask:

"Do you happen to have a bit of a special power?"

"...Huh?"

The woman hiding her face—Ruri Hijiribe—was taken aback. She stared down the Black Rider before her.

Ruri had decided that in order to give her time to think about her future, she ought to return home. But given that she was a very recognizable figure, she couldn't afford to cause a stir around town.

That white man might be lurking around somewhere.

It was a single phone call the previous night that had lured her out as Hollywood.

"I know your secret. Let's go watch a movie together. A monster movie from Hollywood," his message went, along with the location of that park and a time. That was where she met that hit man—and a true monster.

None of it mattered to her now—but according to Yuuhei, there was a good chance that monster was a relative of his.

Perhaps that was why he helped her: a feeling of guilt and responsibility. Meanwhile, Yuuhei introduced this person to her.

He said, "My brother knows a courier who he tells me about all the time. I'll ask him if he can put you in touch." And here she was now, meeting the Black Rider.

The rider was an abnormal being in each and every way—but most surprising to Ruri was the way the rider was able to pinpoint that one feature about her.

That her body might not be entirely human in nature.

$$♂♀$$

Late last night, Russia Sushi

A black-market doctor spoke over the phone with his father.

"So will you explain what's going on here, Dad?"

"...Sometimes coincidence can be detestable. I think I understand how Izaya feels."

"What? Whatever. So how do you and that Russian know each other?"

"...He's, well, something of a handyman. He likes to think of himself as the man whose identity no one knows. So it's quite impressive that Nebula and I have a connection to him. Hopefully, this will impress your father's value upon you."

"So he's a hired killer who likes to puff himself up. Yes?"

"...I don't know how you were raised to be so devoid of joy. But we can set that aside for now. He was hired to abduct a certain woman."

"A woman?"

"Yes... I believe you are aware of the serial killer known as Hollywood?"

"..."

"Nebula was investigating this matter, sensing that, like Celty and Saika, there was some supernatural element at play—and eventually arrived at a woman who had some supernatural blood like Celty's in her family tree a few generations back. This creature lived among mankind and used its power to amass quite a fortune. We're not sure if it was an atavistic trait, or if the qualities were passed through each generation along the way—but at any rate, the power seems to have manifested itself in her. Rather than have the police catch and execute her, we think

it would be better for us to take custody of her, so we can slice and inject and share all that wonderful time together instead. Got it?"

"...Dad, I hope that someday you come to some sobering realizations about yourself."

"Well, that's rather offensive from you, Shinra. But setting that aside...to be honest, Nebula's observer said that she was knocked flat out by a normal civilian, so perhaps she is not worth the trouble of experimenting on. You can just ignore her."

"Hey, would that girl happen to have the name...Ruri Hijiribe?"

"How did you know that?! Shinra, you read my mind! You've been around Celty so long, some of her inhuman power has rubbed off on—beep, beep, beep..."

♂♀

Earlier in the day

Celty dropped off her charge in front of the apartment building and happily typed away into her PDA.

"Pleasure doing business."

I'm glad nothing happened while we were on the road. I guess it wasn't worth freaking out over that bounty thing after all.

If Celty had a nose, she would have been humming. Her client bowed over and over to her.

"Um, th-thank you so much! So, about the money..."

"No, thanks. This one is on the house."

"Huh...?"

"I'm just happy to meet you. I basically never see people like you around the city."

The topic caused a twinge of curiosity in Ruri's heart again.

"Um, when you say that...do you mean...?"

She felt shy about bringing up the subject but summoned up her courage and said, "The things the TV said about you...are they true? You're...not human?"

"Yes. Shall I show you evidence?" the Headless Rider asked, impossibly frank. She removed her helmet, almost proud to show off that she was a monster.

*   *   *

Several minutes later, Celty was gone, and Ruri was back safely in her apartment, standing in front of the mirror, examining her face. It was pale, but not dangerously so.

The throbbing pain all over was gone, a good reminder that her body was not normal.

She twirled a nearby forty-five-pound barbell around with a pinkie finger, a good reminder that her strength was not normal.

She wasn't human.

But she couldn't be a monster, either.

She was *something* in between.

"Ha-ha…"

Until this point, every time she faced that fact, she'd been plunged into a depressive mood…but this time, for some reason, she laughed.

"Aha-ha-ha-ha-ha!"

She laughed loud and heartily, as if it were the first time in her life. She pictured Celty, the Headless Rider, and laughed with tears running down her cheeks.

Oh. So that's how it is.
The world—the world's heart is vast and wide.
Even ghosts and monsters can enjoy life.
Even me, and Yuuhei, and that Headless Rider!
Why…why did I never consider this…?
I've been so stupid!

Several hours later, Ruri's laughter and tears had faded away, and she was flipping through the TV.

On a news program, they were broadcasting a segment about a ten million–yen bounty on a freak in Ikebukuro. Meanwhile, street gangs and bikers from all over were piling into the city in search of the bounty, leading to a very touchy situation.

"…"

She got up and headed into the back of the house—to her changing room.

* * *

Another hour later, Ruri left her home in full costume. Outside were four men whose appearance left no question what they were.

"You must be Ruri Hijiri…what? Wh-wh…what the fuck are you dressed like that for?!"

With a single weak punch to the solar plexus of each, she dispatched the four men quickly. She might have broken a rib here or there, but that wasn't her concern.

The monster known as Hollywood, fully refreshed and renewed, leaped from the fifth floor of her apartment building, her heart soaring like never before—laughing, laughing all the while.

Oddly enough, the sight was reminiscent of a Headless Rider who had raced down the side of a building just a year earlier.

♂♀

At present, tunnel, Ikebukuro

Celty was stunned at the sudden appearance of the thing and slowly turned to face it.

The headless knight turned silently to her and extended a thumb upward.

Before Celty could say anything, the knight said, in hushed tones that only the dullahan could hear, "You did me a favor. Now it's my turn to repay it."

"…"

Celty came to a stop—right as Hollywood, in the form of a headless knight this time, burst into motion.

Her action was entirely unlike Egor's, a mass of metal moving in direct lines. Going easy or not, her first kick blasted a motorcycle into the air, and she carved out the engine with a single hand, using her other hand to block an oncoming metal pipe and twist it.

As she inflicted horrifying fear upon the bikers, Hollywood sang a little song inside her heart. A song just for herself, one she would never sing when she was a star idol.

I am monster, I am human.

I don't care which. I don't care which.
You can't choose your life. Not the start, not the end.
So choose your lifestyle. That's what I choose.
What the courier did for me this morning is worth more than my entire fortune.
Whether I live until tomorrow or live for a thousand years,
as a monster, as a human being,
whether I fight or accept,
I choose to savor.

Hollywood buried her urge to scream within her and raced, raced through the underground tunnel.

The bartender man.

Yuuhei Hanejima.

Celty Sturluson.

She displayed her gratitude and respect for these three monsters—all of whom she'd met in a period of just twenty-four hours—and danced the dance of Hollywood.

♂♀

Celty and the bikers weren't the only ones shocked by the sudden appearance of these monsters. Kadota and his friends, who were about to jump out of the van, and even Mikado and Anri, chasing on foot, were all stopped dead in their tracks by what they saw unfolding.

Two monsters moving in very different ways were neutralizing the motorcycle gangs at a breathless pace. Inside the van, Kadota muttered, "Well, given that these guys are probably all the wimps who weren't allowed to join Toramaru's main force...it's still impressive. What the hell is going on?"

No one could give him an answer.

Unsure quite how to react given the circumstances, Celty settled on just using her shadow ropes to immobilize the bikers. Eventually, the bandaged man was back at her side. He whispered haltingly into her ear, "Hurry, take care, of Mother."

Mother?

She looked back at him, momentarily confused, then understood his meaning at once. Through the gaps in his bandages, she saw that the man's eyes were red and bloodshot.

Saika?!

Celty spun around to find Anri standing at the entrance to the tunnel, looking troubled. She confirmed that the two monsters nearby were more than enough to handle the situation, and also weren't going too far in their violence, and decided—despite still not fully understanding the circumstances—that she could leave the scene to them and escape.

She quickly crafted a message on her PDA and used an extended shadow to show it to both of the monsters.

"Let me give you two pieces of advice."

She didn't realize that both pieces would come off as extremely ironic to her audience.

"If you see a cop on a bike, just run away. One of them is a real monster."

These two pieces of advice were the most crucial things Celty could think to impart.

"The other thing, which you might have already heard about..."

The problem was, her warning was just a day too late.

"Never pick a fight with a guy in a bartender's uniform. Never!"

♂♀

Celty sent a safety signal to Kadota's group and left the danger zone. With Anri at her back and Mikado dragged into the van, they left the tunnel behind.

She undid her shadow net at the very end, but it had already served its purpose. All of the gangsters and their bikes were on the run from the two monsters.

As he watched from a distance, Aoba Kuronuma tilted his head in confusion and wondered, "Um...what just happened?"

But the twins behind him couldn't answer. They looked at each other, equally confused.

Ultimately, no single person involved in the bizarre incident understood the full context of it.

♂♀

A few minutes later

The bikers, fleeing with their tails between their legs, sneakily made their way through the neighborhood to avoid the motorcycle cops. From what they heard over their walkie-talkies, many of their friends had already been hauled in.

"Shit...now we can't even go back home... The chief'll kill us."

One of the men in a striped gang uniform, apparently the leader of the expedition, called out to the fifteen or so members still remaining. The police would spot them in minutes if they moved as a full group, but they didn't have enough power left to implement a better plan.

"We at least gotta show off our power to a local gang to regain some face..."

They forgot about their own damage and headed off through the town, driven by their twisted desire to express themselves through violence. And when they got to a street close to the Sunshine building, they found what looked like local thugs and stopped their bikes on a side road to play tough.

"Hey, you. Got a question for ya. What's the name of the team that reps this area?"

One of the local toughs thought it over and gave them an answer.

"There's a bunch around here... For the more organized types, you want the Jan-Jaka-Jan who work for the Awakusu-kai. For the street racers, I guess it'd be the Dragon Zombies? But ever since that crazy motor cop showed up, they're all keeping it on the DL."

"Awright. You tell me where to go to find 'em, then."

"You going to fight 'em?"

"Fuck's it to ya?!" the leader in ritual garb demanded. The local thug shook his head.

"You guys are in Toramaru from Saitama, right? C'mon, you know your boss doesn't like this kinda stuff, right? The guy might be a womanizer, but I've heard he's at least got some honor."

"Shuddup! Chief's got nothin' to do with this!"

"We were supposed to catch that Black Rider and get the money, then pass it up the chain so we could go independent!"

"Come on… You're gonna get ten million yen for nothing, then give it to the yakuza? Seriously? If I got my hands on that kind of cash, I'd use it for myself. You wouldn't need to be a biker at all with that kind of money. You want to ride, just get your own tuned-up wheels," the dreadlocked thug advised, whether he was saying it out of sarcasm or honest helpfulness.

"What…? You dissin' us like we're a buncha *penkoro*?! Huh?!"

As outsiders to the city, there was very little concern about fights with the locals following them back home. So without that threat in the back of their minds, frustration had no brakes to keep it from spilling into anger and violence.

"What's a *penkoro*?"

"Tom, forget about them and let's go. I'm getting hungry."

"Yeah, good point. I just wish the boss would buy us dinner once in a while…"

The local toughs' utter indifference to them pushed the bikers over the edge.

"You bitches… Don't ignore us!"

One of them pulled off a metal pipe that was affixed to his bike and swung it with all his might.

"Whoa, watch out!" said the dreadlocked man, cleanly dodging the blow.

But just as a metal pipe had ripped through Celty's cargo bag earlier in the day—it ripped through the other thug's *bartender-style sleeve*.

"Ah!"

"My clothes…," the man said quietly.

The one with dreads was already sprinting away, signing the cross as he prayed for the bikers.

The next instant: *zwip*.

If there were visible sound effects in real life, that's what would appear over the scene: *zwip*.

That was how easily the man picked up the motorcycle, rider and all, with one hand.

And like tossing a baseball, threw it into the other bikers.

*   *   *

You see, the outsiders did not realize.

That in Ikebukuro, there are people *one must never pick a fight with*.

People that no one should ever, ever, ever challenge to a fight, no matter if they were a hit man, or a serial killer, or a president, or an alien, or a vampire, or a headless monster.

Then came the sound of thunder.

"You ripped the clothes...I got from Kasukaaaa!"

The man in the bartender getup pulled out a nearby streetlamp and swung it at the bikers like a baseball bat.

There was the sound of thunder, and both motorcycles and men flew through the air.

With that customary sight, Ikebukuro's holiday came to an end.

Whether the city enjoyed its holiday or not is not for us to know.

But at the very least...

The neighborhood of Ikebukuro was at peace again today.

EPILOGUE

Epilogue 1: Secret Conversation

Chat room

Izaya Orihara returns to life!
Izaya Orihara: I want to ask you something about the motorcycle gang incident and what happened with Celty.
Shinichi Tsukumoya: Ah, there you are. Welcome.
Izaya Orihara: No need for greetings... So what ultimately happened there?
Shinichi Tsukumoya: You weren't actively involved in that? I'm surprised.
Izaya Orihara: Come on, don't tease me. I'll make this worth your while.
Shinichi Tsukumoya: Ha-ha! We can discuss price later. As a matter of fact, I'm itching to discuss it, too.
Izaya Orihara: I know the Awakusu-kai were involved somehow. I just don't know what they're after.
Shinichi Tsukumoya: Ah yes. They were trying to get rid of someone. So to make it easier, they brought in some *bosozoku* motorcycle gangs from out of town to raise hell. The person they wanted to erase would cause a big stir if missing, see.
Izaya Orihara: Who?

Shinichi Tsukumoya: Ruri Hijiribe. You've heard that name before, haven't you?

Izaya Orihara: I have. What kind of joke is this?

Shinichi Tsukumoya: Joke? Please. Have you grown so soft that you can't even tell truthful info from lies? What are you, a rival character who suddenly pales in comparison when a new story arc begins? Should I call you Yamcha Orihara now?

Izaya Orihara: Who was the client?

Shinichi Tsukumoya: Jinnai Yodogiri, the representative director of Yodogiri Shining Corporation.

Izaya Orihara: And why would he need to kill his best asset?

Shinichi Tsukumoya: Dunno. You know I don't pry into matters like that, don't you?

Izaya Orihara: ...

Shinichi Tsukumoya: But Yodogiri made one mistake. Going to the Awakusu-kai was the right idea, but it ended up being seen as betrayal by the Awakusu.

Izaya Orihara: Ohh...?

Shinichi Tsukumoya: You see, telling them to finish off a target without revealing that the target was Hollywood is akin to sending those men to their deaths. Now President Yodogiri is missing, and his talent agency is in a total state of chaos.

♂♀

Jack-o'-Lantern Japan Talent Agency Office, Higashi-Nakano

Ultimately, Ikebukuro was full of people searching for the Black Rider for several days after that, not just the first chaotic twenty-four hours. On top of that, the appearance of a look-alike "headless knight" only added to the confusion.

The hassle was worth more than the increased shopping and tourism the event brought with it, so the police eventually succeeded in getting the bounty withdrawn.

The publicity costs for all the billboards announcing the nullification

of the bounty and the subsequent apologies to the public were stagger-
ing, but the president of Jack-o'-Lantern Japan was all smiles.

"Fantastic... Hey! Let's hear some applause! I am damn fantastic right now, folks! Applause! I can't hear you! More applause with
the cheers and the clapping! It's a celebration! I am celebrating
you right now! To hell with the scandals and whatnot—I celebrate
you two!"

Several days after the incident, amid a barrage of thirty firecrackers
courtesy of the agency president, stood an expressionless male star
and a gloomy but beautiful female star.

They had no way of knowing how, but Ruri Hijiribe's agency president, Yodogiri, had vanished under mysterious circumstances. The
agency went into panic mode, and Ruri Hijiribe was the first asset to
change hands—to Jack-o'-Lantern Japan.

There were a number of initial theories about the disappear-
ance, one of which even posited that he was so shocked by the scandal with Yuuhei Hanejima that he wandered into the woods and
vanished.

But because he was not a man with a good reputation to begin with,
society quickly accepted the change and began to celebrate Ruri Hijiribe's new start.

After President Max Sandshelt happily, liberally complimented
himself and his company, he said something about "leaving the
rest up to the young lovers" and took the managers away for a
meeting.

Kanemoto, the temporary manager, ended up taking off work from
the physical stress of Yuuhei's scandal coming out on his watch—but
that's a story for another time.

The two actors were left alone.

It was silent between them. Their so-called romance had been a
sham meant to help them get through a perilous situation. Ruri eventually broke the silence, grinning faintly as she turned to the typically
expressionless Yuuhei.

"Um...there are things...I haven't told you, aren't there...?"

"Like what?"

"...Like how I discovered my Hollywood power...and why I became a killer...and what...Yodogiri and them...did to me."

She was smiling, but her voice quavered faintly. No matter what the blood within her said, she was clearly reliving the memories that drove her peaceful life to one of murder.

Without moving a muscle in his face, Yuuhei said, "If you don't want to talk about it, you shouldn't force yourself."

"I want you...to hear it."

"I refuse," he said conclusively, a rare thing for him. The serial killer woman flinched. To her surprise, he was as flat and straightforward as ever as he said, "Once you tell me your story, you're going to kill yourself, aren't you?"

"..."

Her silence was all the confirmation he needed.

"Listen, Ruri. I'm not the tree that you tell the secret of the king's ears to." As usual, it was impossible to tell if he was angrily chiding her or not. "I'm just a human, as you can see... I thought, if I can't understand others, I should at least make the effort to try...and I've been watching ever since."

"..."

"So I'm pretty sure I know what you're thinking. As usual, I don't know what you're feeling, but I understand your thoughts. I don't want you to die, Ruri. So don't tell me anything."

"...Maybe you really are a monster," she said out of admiration, not disgust. "When I was a girl...I wanted to destroy absolutely everything. But...more than that, I was just afraid of losing what was around me. I wasn't able to be a monster...not to the extent of completely ruining myself. I think that, ultimately, I was most afraid of losing myself."

"Losing is scary. I suppose you could say that's a form of love."

If he'd said it with a grin, it would have come across as cocky and cool, but the flat monotone of Yuuhei's voice actually gave the words a strange impact.

When silence crept between them again, it was Yuuhei who broke it this time.

"...There's one thing I didn't say."

"What is it?"

"Back in my room, when you knocked me over and sat on top—I'm pretty sure I was panicking."

"...Huh?"

If she had swung her arm down on him, he would have died without making a sound—of that, Ruri was certain. This was a baffling thing to admit. She looked closer.

Yuuhei stared back into her eyes, and for just an instant, he looked troubled.

"My pulse got faster, and my chest felt hot."

"..."

"..."

"Are you...trying to hit on me?"

"I'm only speaking the truth," the perfect man said, perplexed.

Ruri laughed. "You're just like a child, Yuuhei."

And she smiled, not with the shadowy wan smile of earlier, but an innocent, childish grin of her own. The girl who had been a serial killer mumbled, "But...I don't really mind that."

♂♀

Chat room

Izaya Orihara: Well, what about the murder-machine, then? Why would that hit man help Celty out?

Shinichi Tsukumoya: ...Wow, you really were out of the loop on this one. Has Ikebukuro abandoned you?

Izaya Orihara: What do you mean?

Shinichi Tsukumoya: I mean...that was all caused by your own sisters, you know that?

Izaya Orihara: What?

♂♀

Sunshine, Sixtieth Floor Street, Ikebukuro

One evening a few days after the incident, Kururi and Mairu were out on a shopping trip, with Egor tagging along behind them as the pack mule. The bandaged man was carrying a huge number of bags from department stores for the twin girls, wondering, "You have so many clothes already, and now you buy more?"

"...We're just...getting started."

"No complaining, Egor! We fronted your treatment money, and you just let Celty get away from us!"

They had picked up a lost bag of money and were using it to curry favors, a truly brazen decision. On the other hand, who knew how the law would treat cash lost by a nonhuman being? Still, they were undeniably guilty of using someone else's money.

"Forgive me for speaking out of turn, mistress," the hit man said smoothly, bowing with a hint of sarcasm, but Mairu didn't mind. She grinned toothily.

"Well, whatever! I do forgive you! In a way, those biker gangs were chasing after us! And we can claim that we saved you from it! So thank us! Special thanks! Canadian thanks!" she babbled nonsensically, puffing up her chest with pride. Kururi sighed and thwomped her.

"Ouch!!"

"...Don't be...stuck up."

The hit man straightened up and resumed following the sisters.

In conclusion, Kururi and Mairu's actions could all be explained as an extension of a simple desire: to see the Black Rider and expose its identity.

They picked up an envelope belonging to the Black Rider. Based on a certain source of information, they learned that the name Celty on the envelope belonged to a courier who manipulated the Black Rider, and so they put a plan into motion.

In exchange for the medical funds, they had the staff of Russia Sushi put on a little act for them. The manager hid his face and made contact with Celty, along with the bag containing Egor hidden inside. When they reached either Celty's base or a resting point, Egor would contact the twins' phone—according to the plan.

It didn't seem right to ask an injured man to do this, but Egor claimed that he was "good at that sort of thing" and took the lead in accepting the job.

In truth, if they wanted to meet Celty, they could have just asked Simon, and he would arrange a meeting—but Simon himself assumed this was some kind of prank, thus setting up the twins' grand Celty-capturing plan on a one-way trip to failure.

In other words, for the simple purpose of meeting someone, they set up a complex, dead-end plan that used up all of the million yen they found.

Ultimately, all of that money found its way back to Celty's household.

"So in the end, the one who caught all those bikers in the tunnel under the train tracks was Egor? Isn't that crazy? I knew you were something special, so I guess you must be some kind of Russian super-soldier! You should come to my dojo sometime!"

"…That's amazing."

"No…it was thanks to someone else."

This was how Ikebukuro's greatest troublemakers gained the troubling tool of violence—but they didn't really think much of it at the time. They stared at each other.

Two souls in love who spent very different lives in their desire to return to one being.

"Anyway, let's buy the ingredients for tonight's stew and go home! You should eat dinner with us, too, Egor!"

"…Well, I won't be in business for a while. If you don't mind my company…"

"…Shabu-shabu."

Even these girls with their many contradictions were welcomed silently into the city's embrace.

As if the city itself desired a fresh new breeze to run within it.

♂♀

Chat room

Izaya Orihara: So in the end…the murder-machine and the serial killer had nothing to do with Celty, and they both helped rescue her…

Shinichi Tsukumoya: It's ironic. And the one who first sent them down that path was your good friend Shizuo.

Izaya Orihara: ...

Shinichi Tsukumoya: Don't sulk at me. Ikebukuro enjoyed its holiday. It's a good thing you were over in Shinjuku and had nothing to do with it!

Izaya Orihara: Are you still going on about that nonsense?

Shinichi Tsukumoya: As usual, you love people, but you won't acknowledge that neighborhoods have their own character.

Izaya Orihara: I don't want to talk about occult nonsense.

Shinichi Tsukumoya: That's not how it is. See, a city has numerous memes... Well, in this case, they're human beings acting as brain cells. They come together, and the reactions of those cells are what creates the mind of the city. Each cell is meaningless on its own. It's the exchanges that actually give a city its character, so it can enjoy its holiday.

Izaya Orihara: I understand the logic, but I have no interest in this. I'm leaving for now.

Shinichi Tsukumoya: Be careful not to get punched by Shizuo. Or Simon.

Izaya Orihara: Just remember, one of these days I'm going to find your real address.

Izaya Orihara confirmed dead!

Shinichi Tsukumoya: As I'm sure you know, I'm in this chat room twenty-four hours a day.

Shinichi Tsukumoya's turn!
Shinichi Tsukumoya's turn!
Shinichi Tsukumoya's turn!
Shinichi Tsukumoya's turn!
Shinichi Tsukumoya's turn!
Shinichi Tsukumoya's turn!

Shinichi Tsukumoya's turn!

Shinichi Tsukumoya's turn!

Shinichi Tsukumoya's turn!
.
.
.

Epilogue 2: Roundtable Conversation

Along Kawagoe Highway, Ikebukuro

"All right, is everyone paying attention? *Sagohachi*-style means 'three-five-eight,' and that refers to the ratio of the pickling ingredients! You create the fermentation base using three parts salt, five parts koji yeast, and eight parts rice! That's all it takes, but it's the magic ingredient that will help you make all kinds of food!"

This excited cooking commentary was coming from a girl with a scar on her neck and a pink apron with "Seiji Love" written on the front—the stalker, Mika Harima.

Celty couldn't help but feel slightly wrong as she watched the girl wearing her own face executing a perfect meal.

Her bounty was gone, and she was taking advantage of her newly returned freedom to take cooking classes. She had reached out to Anri first, but Anri said that she couldn't cook, either. Next was Karisawa, who was good with her hands, but it was revealed that she had no skill with traditional Japanese cooking.

Celty's ultimate goal was to cook *sagohachi*-style pickled sandfish, so she needed someone who could handle traditional cooking—and of all people, Anri brought her to Mika.

Naturally, Seiji Yagiri tagged along. When he saw Celty, he asked, "You aren't searching for your head anymore?" When she nodded to indicate this was the case, he seemed oddly emboldened and said, "Guess I gotta search on my own, then..."

Celty could tell that Mika was listening in on that one-sided conversation, which made the dullahan feel rather uncomfortable. On the other hand, she had to admit that Mika's cooking was first-rate.

With just a few fancy knife flourishes for some little appetizers, Mika finished up the fermentation base for Celty's long-awaited *sagohachi* dish. Excited about the prospect of serving dinner to everyone, Celty had made sure to buy some fish on the way to the lesson, but it wasn't that simple.

"Okay! Now we just put the fish in here and let it sit overnight!"

Overnight...?

Once she realized that it meant there was no dinner for that evening, Shinra smacked a fist into his palm and said, "Let's have a stew."

"We can call everyone we know to come over and have a hot pot party."

♂♀

Meat, meat, veggies, meat, veggies
  Meat, meat, veggies, meat, veggies
  Tofu in sesame sauce, veggies in ponzu
  The fat level determines what goes on the meat.

If there was any poetic description for the state of the apartment, it was these four bars from an old commercial. That was how lustily they tore into the hot pot.

On the top floor of a luxury apartment building along Kawagoe Highway, the massive dining area was so full of heat that it seemed cramped. About ten people were seated around a large table, which featured two portable gas stoves bearing equally large stew pots.

It was a varied group crowded around the pots, from students in uniform to a man in a bartender's outfit to a Caucasian woman.

"All right, we've got some more meat coming up!" said a grinning young woman bearing a large tray and wearing an apron fashioned out of a body-pillow cover with a manga character on it. What ensued was a thoroughly impolite chopstick battle for control of the goods.

But one person sat on the sofa in the living room on the other side of the dining area, observing the fray. The observer was in a thorough state of relaxation, but there was one abnormality about its silhouette.

The black shadow with legs crossed on the sofa had no head above the neck.

A young man in a white coat sat down next to the figure. Despite the lack of a head, the black shadow pulled out a PDA and began to type a message.

"You aren't going to eat?"

"I'm full just from seeing you smile," he said, an odd statement to a person without a face.

The shadow shrugged slightly and typed out, *"Don't mind me. Thanks, though."*

The young man looked at the text and smiled shyly. Over the raucous sounds of the nearby shabu-shabu party, he said, "These last few days have been very wild."

"I guess."

"Let's see… Should I start with the kinky abandonment I suffered…?"

"Don't call it kinky abandonment!"

By putting her hands around his neck, Celty inadvertently returned the apartment to its most customary state. But suddenly, she stopped, acting seriously, and asked, *"What do you suppose I should have done?"*

"About what?"

"Everything ended without any real answers. I just…don't know if I should continue with my courier work or not…"

"What's this all about?"

"If I take on some dangerous job, it could mean bad news for you, even if I'm not—" she began to write, when Shinra reached out and closed the PDA screen.

"Like I said earlier, we're a family now, so a bit of trouble means nothing to me… And as long as I'm scaling that wall with you, no difficulty is a bad thing to me."

" … "

"Don't you realize I've already scaled the highest wall there is—getting you to love me?" the doctor stated boldly and shamelessly. Celty smiled inwardly, picked up the nearby helmet, and bumped its visor against his forehead.

And so the doting lovers, as well as all the people sitting around the table, heartily savored their happiness in whatever form it took.

As members of one giant family within the context of a city, they found the places they could call their own within their daily lives.

It was as though the city, after enjoying its holiday, decided to give a little something back.

♂♀

"Man, I really made a lot of money that day. Not much of it made sense, but I got eight hundred thousand yen up front. The funny thing is, the

cargo ended up moving on his own. Should I assume that I actually did the job they paid me for?"

"As long as there are no complaints, right? I went through a lot of trouble that night, but I made two hundred thousand yen on my own."

"Ooh! That makes a million yen...the exact amount that I lost! We made it back!"

"Way to go, Celty! It is a triumph of the power of our love!"

As a matter of fact, that money was the very same stack of bills that Celty had lost to begin with, which meant that she and Shinra had essentially done a very busy day's work for free.

But whether they ever realized that or not is a story for another time.

♂♀

Chat room

TarouTanaka: By the way, I had a hot pot with some friends today.
Setton: What a coincidence. So did I.
Kanra: What?! You had a hot pot? At this time of year?!
Kuru: Why, how coincidental! We, too, enjoyed some delicious shabu-shabu on this day!
Mai: It was yummy.

<Private Mode> Kanra: Oh, you're here again.
<Private Mode> Kanra: You, too? Where did you have this party? You have friends to enjoy a hot pot with?
<Private Mode> Kuru: Oh my goodness.
<Private Mode> Kuru: I wish that you would not pry into the matters of a young girl and her friendships, Brother.

Mai: It's a secret.
TarouTanaka: ?

<Private Mode> Kanra: Dammit, Mairu, would you just learn how to use private mode already?!

*   *   *

Bacura: I went with a female friend of mine to go eat sukiyaki. You know that place with all-you-can-eat sukiyaki for just 1,500 yen?

TarouTanaka: Oh yeah, it's a chain!

Saika: i had the hot pot with setton. it was good

Kanra: Good grief, is anyone keeping up with the season?

Kanra: All those stews and hot pots are meant for the winter only!

♂♀

Izaya's apartment, Shinjuku

"Hey, Namie."

"What?"

Izaya stopped staring at his desktop and turned with a smile to Namie, who was busy completing work tasks on her laptop.

"Feel like having a hot pot? Shabu-shabu, crab stew—anything you want."

"Would you mind not using me to fulfill your empty sense of vanity, just because your chat room friends are all having hot pots?" Namie responded.

Izaya's cheek twitched, and he shook his head. "…Did you see that?"

"The whole thing."

"I see… You were the one who told my sisters about Celty, weren't you?"

"That's a good question. Oh, look…your weird girlie talk online is even creepier than before," Namie said with an evil grin and derisive glance toward Izaya, as she monitored the chat room on her laptop in between tasks. "Also, I'm surprised… It turns out you have a human side after all. Perhaps that's the eternal twenty-one-year-old in you?"

"You are developing into quite a handful… Shit, I should have made it invisible to anyone outside of the participants, the way Tsukumoya's is set up," he grumbled. The so-called puppet master, who had been outside of the loop this entire time, looked out of the window.

Izaya gazed upon the profile of Shinjuku and thought to himself.

He had abandoned any pretense at a normalized life that brought stability and relief.

He did not find it necessary for himself, but he understood that people did need such a thing.

He envied the members of the chat who fondly spoke of their lives, looked out the window at the sky, and envied Ikebukuro itself.

The city swallowed that one man's envy and sang the glories of its holiday once again.

Next Prologue

Once he had thoroughly envied Ikebukuro's holiday, Izaya shut his eyes and smiled.

"Yes…I suppose I should enjoy my holiday now."

The man who had been left out of all the fun this time smiled with vengeance.

"There are plenty of sparks…that might be put to use."

♂♀

The night of the incident

When she was under the blanket, Anri quietly thought to herself. She thought of the bandaged man who had helped Celty earlier in the day.

His face was covered by those bandages…but I'm sure of it. That was him.

The white man who had been talking to the man in the gas mask while they were returning from karaoke the night before.

The memory of that sighting caused Anri to pull the blanket up over her head so she could face the curse echoing throughout her body.

When he had been talking to the man in the gas mask, she felt a hand on her shoulder from behind—and in that moment, a nasty sense of pressure engulfed her entire body.

A cold sharpness ran through her shoulder, and for a moment, time froze within her.

It felt like her freedom of movement had been stolen, like her body was being manhandled all over.

Zig-zig-zig-zig-zig-zig-zig—

The march of the ugly creaking reached its peak, and every cell in her body screamed.

Warning her of the danger of the man behind her.

That he was far, far more dangerous than she could imagine.

*　　*　　*

Which was why she needed to love him that very instant.

In that moment, it was not the man's presence that was handling her.

The creaking, the *zig-zig-zigging* inside her body was Saika itself.

The moment the hand landed on Anri's shoulder, only she was aware of what happened.

Every cell in her body screamed out, and Saika's true body emerged, just the tip, from her shoulder, slicing the palm of the hand that had been placed there.

As a result, the man became a child of Saika's and not by Anri's choice.

Even knowing that it would not affect his daily life, even knowing that he was not working in an honest trade, Anri could not ignore the shock of having inflicted that curse upon him.

What if...

What if, just like today...Saika activates and does the same thing to Ryuugamine or Kida...?

The realization that the curse she had come to accept was far more dangerous than she was giving it credit for plunged Anri into a state of fear.

Not fear that she would be taken over by Saika—but fear that she might use Saika to control those she loved. And in the background, she heard the quiet voices cursing.

Cursing her with their love, over and over and over.

♂♀

A conversation between three Russians in their mother tongue, Russia Sushi

"All right, Egor. You're Colonel Lingerin's right-hand man...so if you're here, what happened?"

"We've got two men AWOL from the organization."

"Ha-ha! You mean us? You're coming to finish us off, after all this time?"

"No… Colonel Lingerin has no desire to deal with you at this point. The escapees are two others that you wouldn't know…"

"They're apparently hiding out in Tokyo, so I thought I would let you two know. And now thanks to my desire to engage in a little side business, I've had to get plastic surgery."

♂♀

A conversation between officers of the Awakusu-kai

"So…we still can't find Yodogiri?"
"…The other families seem to think that we took him out."
"To think that old badger was in bed with multiple yakuza groups… We took him for granted."
"You can't be too careful. He's more than just the president of a talent agency… There's too much there that doesn't add up."
"…So the fact that he put us head-to-head with Hollywood means we were nothing but sacrificial pawns to him?"
"The bastard."
"Spare no expense on intel. I want that fraud to sleep with the fishes."

♂♀

A conversation between boys, Ikebukuro

"Mr. Ryuugamine's really fascinating. Yeah, he's so interesting. He might even be more interesting as a friend than Mr. Kida."
"On what basis?" "Great, there goes your sickness again." "Hee-hee!"
"I told you about how we got attacked by the motorcycle gangs while riding in a van, right?"
"Weren't you the one who called in one of those gangs, Izumii?"
"Don't call me by my old name. It makes me think of my brother."
"Must be weird for brothers to have different last names. But I bet you're happy not to share a name with a brother stuck in juvie, huh?"
"You know what my older brother did? He took the Blue Squares I went to all the trouble of creating and ruined them. Useless idiot."

"So what's this Mr. Ryuugamine like? You make it sound like he'll be real useful."

"…Oh, right. Yeah… Anyway, we were stuck in this obviously crazy situation, where anyone would break down in tears… But Mr. Ryuugamine…he was *smiling* about it."

"Seriously?" "He a masochist?" "Hee-hee!"

"That's what I mean—He's real fascinating. I think he loves it."

"Loves what?"

"He's one of those people… He just loves stuff that's estranged from reality, like it came straight out of a manga—even if it's deadly dangerous. That's why…I think Mr. Ryuugamine created the Dollars."

"I don't get it." "What does estranged mean?" "Dude, you are so dumb."

"I'll knock you out!" "Hee-hee!"

"Quit fighting… Anyway, the fight between the Yellow Scarves and the Dollars was just getting good—and then it ended without much of a fuss. That's no fun, right?"

"So you're gonna start a new spark of conflict, Aoba?"

"Yeah, except…someone's trying to scoop it up from the side and use it for himself. Who we ought to be dealing with first is that hyena…Izaya Orihara."

"Any means necessary?"

"Just one thing: Don't mess with his two sisters. I like them. Remember what I said about those girls who just kissed me out of nowhere?"

"…I'll kill you!"

"Ow-ow-ow-ow, knock it off, asshole! You know the reason you don't get any girls is because you take stuff like that seriously… Ow-ow-ow-ow-ow-ow! Stop! Something just snapped! I heard something snap inside of me—ow-ow-ow-ow-ow-ow-ow!"

"Hey, watch out, Kuronuma's gonna die." "C'mon, let's just kill him now." "Hee-hee!"

♂♀

"There are always sparks, everywhere."

Izaya smiled to himself and began to monologue in front of Namie.

"What I do is pinch a few of them—then release them all in one place."

A look of bliss came over the info agent's features as he imagined the sparks igniting a real fire.

"And then I'll tell this *city* something it needs to hear."

With great pleasure, and just a touch of hatred, drunk on himself and with a note of self-reassurance, Izaya said:

"Holiday's over, motherfucker."

Like us, the city wants to take a holiday sometimes.

I'm pretty sure I said that before.

So what does it do when the holiday is over?

It returns to a normal schedule, of course. At that point, it naturally won't have time to watch you anymore.

After all, only when it has plenty of time does the city toy with its people.

So you see, even if Ikebukuro were locked in a dire, desperate situation, the city will cut its losses. It won't save you. It says, you should just run to the police.

For you see, once the city returns to normal, it won't even notice your situation.

But don't forget: You are also a part of the city.

And as part of the city, you must simply do what you should, with all your strength.

If you do, then someday the city will wish to rest once more.

I pray that we meet again.

May the city celebrate your holiday…

—Excerpt from the afterword of Shinichi Tsukumoya, author of Media Wax's Ikebukuro travel guide, *Ikebukuro Strikes Back II*

Shizuo Heiwajima
Simon Brezhnev

Masaomi Kida
Mika Harima
Seiji Yagiri

Shingen Kishitani
Emilia

Shiki
Tom Tanaka
Kinnosuke Kuzuhara
Shinichi Tsukumoya

STAFF

Author
Ryohgo Narita

Illustrations & Visual Concepts
Suzuhito Yasuda (AWA Studio)

Design
Yoshihiko Kamabe

Editing
Sue Suzuki
Atsushi Wada

Publishing
ASCII Media Works

Distribution
Kadokawa Shoten

AFTERWORD

Hello, all you *Durarara!!* readers, it's been a while. I'm Ryohgo Narita.

This story is a peek at the everyday lives of the characters, a bit of a breather between bigger stories. Next time out I hope to deliver much more ominous developments.

When I set out to write this book, my schedule ended up overlapping with about four other deadlines. In essence, this made for the last three days before submission being all-nighters, and after a full night's sleep, I had blood in my urine, and as I'm writing this afterword, my stomach is killing me. That's how bad it was.

I'm slowly recovering now, except for my stomach, but I realize that at this pace, I won't last, and I'm going to take a few months' break before resuming with my next book... I'm sorry about that.

As for my other series, *Baccano!*, its anime is currently re-airing on demand, the Net, and satellite broadcast. By the time this book comes out, there should be a Nintendo DS game as well. I wrote a story that would be the equivalent of nearly a third of one of these volumes, so if you're interested, check that out along with the anime and original novels.

For my future plans, I'll be visiting a doctor if I don't start feeling better soon—but aside from that, I'll be rotating between *Vamp!*, *5656!*, *Baccano! 1710*, then *Durarara!!*, hopefully with some "Hariyama-san at the Center of the World" short stories. I feel bad for slowing things down for readers who only follow one series, but hey, if it gets you to try out one of my other works...

Lastly, my usual thanks.

To all the people in Dengeki's editorial office who okayed various scheduling insanities, the people at the printer's, the proofreaders, and my editor Mr. Papio, who even came in on his days off to work with me.

To Kazuma Kamachi and Mamizu Arisawa, for endorsing my references to their work, and to many other authors for their advice, including Makoto Sanda and Suzu Suzuki.

To the staff of Smile Café Roots, for allowing me to use them in the story.

And to friends, acquaintances, and family.

To Suzuhito Yasuda, for putting up with my last-second schedule, reading the whole story, and providing appropriate illustrations.

And most of all, to you readers.

Thank you so much!

I hope to see you in Ikebukuro's odd daily life again!

Ryohgo Narita